The Four Dorothys

DRAMA!

The Four Dorothys

Don't miss the next show!

DRAMA!
The Four Dorothys

Paul Ruditis

Simon Pulse
NEW YORK   LONDON   TORONTO   SYDNEY

SIMON PULSE

An imprint of Simon & Schuster Children's Publishing Division

1230 Avenue of the Americas, New York, NY 10020

Copyright © 2007 by Paul Ruditis

All rights reserved, including the right of reproduction in whole
.or in part in any form.

SIMON PULSE and colophon are registered trademarks
of Simon & Schuster, Inc.

Designed by Mike Rosamilia

The text of this book was set in Weiss.

Manufactured in the United States of America

First Simon Pulse edition February 2007

4 6 8 10 9 7 5 3

Library of Congress Control Number 2006928449

ISBN-13: 978-1-4169-3391-5

ISBN-10: 1-4169-3391-3

☆ For Jean and Tim ☆

Anything Goes

It was a drag queen's worst nightmare.

There were four of them onstage . . . high school girls, that is, not drag queens. Though I guess some people would say there wasn't much difference between the two.

Each girl was in a pale blue gingham dress and a pair of bright red ruby-esque slippers looking like Dorothy from *The Wizard of Oz*. If they had been drag queens and all four of them showed up wearing the same outfit, looking like their icon, Judy Garland, in her signature ingenue role, I can just imagine the catfight: gingham, sequins, and little stuffed Totos flying *everywhere*.

It was no accident that these girls were dressed (more or less) alike. They were at the final costume fitting for the Orion Academy Spring Theatrical Production of *The Wizard of Oz*. It was the first time the director had a chance to see them all onstage in costume. I suspect he was as surprised by the result as I was. Even though the girls were each playing the same role, they looked nothing alike. Each costume was dramatically different from the next.

But that was the *least* of the issues we were dealing with on this show.

"Bring up the spotlight," Mr. Randall, the drama teacher-director-choreographer, yelled to the stage manager at the back of the auditorium.

Within moments, the Thomas Reed Spotlight lit up the Scott Vanowen Stage in the Saundra Hall Auditorium. My school is big on naming things after people, especially people who are big on making monetary donations to the school. Which is how we wound up with an auditorium that we refer to as Hall Hall.

Maybe someday when I'm a famous alumnus I'll pay to have something named after me. Like an extra wing on the school. Or maybe an entire building. Then again, knowing my luck, there would be a paperwork mix-up and they'd wind up cutting the ribbon on the Bryan Stark Janitorial Closet.

That's me, by the way: Bryan Stark. I tend to think of myself as a supporting character or a background player. My friends take the starring roles. It's not that I plan it that way. It just happens. In the cast list of my life, my name would be somewhere near the bottom.

Don't get me wrong. I don't really mind being in the background when it comes to the day-to-day. Who wants the harsh spotlight of teen drama shining brightly on him, anyway? In the background, I get to watch . . . and critique. I mean, what's the fun of seeing your friends' lives spiral out of control if you can't get in a snarkastic comment or two along the way?

Judgmental? Yes. But I'm okay with that.

That's enough about me for now. I think it's time to set the scene.

Orion Academy is the ultraexclusive (unless your parents have enough money to make it a bit *less* exclusive) high school that I go to. The student population is a little over two hundred of the best and the brightest from the livin'-is-easy beach community of Malibu, CA. We're only thirty minutes from Hollywood, but light-years away from reality.

My school is as much a character in this little drama as the flesh-and-blood cast members I'll be introducing shortly. In many ways, Orion is like any other school in America and yet, totally unique at the same time. I mean, how many other schools were built by a student of the famed architect Frank Lloyd Wright and have—among other interesting features—a waterfall in the lobby? How many have a fully functional observatory on campus? Sit on the edge of a bluff overlooking the Pacific Ocean?

Actually . . . forget what I said about Orion being like any other school in America. That was folly. Pure and utter folly.

Usually, I try to ignore the perks of our school and focus on the realities. Like at that moment the *reality* was the show was opening in one week and we were nowhere near where we needed to be.

The spring production is usually one of the highlights of the year. An amazing performance showcasing some of the best student work this side of the Great White Way. (*Aside:* That's Broadway, for those of you not in the know.)

This year? Not so much.

First of all, you should know that the Orion Theater Department is kind of famous. It helps that the sons and daughters of the biggest movers and shakers in Hollywood go here. That's not to say that they're *all* great actors. Far from it. But when the children of the glitterati decide to follow in Mommy's and Daddy's footsteps . . . well, it's the only school show that regularly appears on *Entertainment Tonight.* The acting may not always be Oscar material, but the buzz is worth its weight in platinum.

This production was different from the regular extravaganza of past years for a few reasons. First off, there was the play.

Now, don't get me wrong, I'm a big fan of *Wizard,* but doesn't that seem a bit more middle school? Or elementary school, even? Shouldn't high school students be over dressing up like a lion, a tin man, or a scarecrow by now? Aren't there, like, a hundred more mature plays to perform?

Grease, at the very least?

The problem was that last year, Mr. Randall, took the spring semester off for a sabbatical. So, a guest director was brought in. Things kind of went all farcical from that point on.

Being Orion Academy, we couldn't just have *any* substitute teacher. The headmaster invited former Tony Award nominee Grayson McDonough in as our sub. Mr. McD (as he forced us to call him) is the same man who produced a revival of the musical 1776 where acrobatic circus clowns played the roles of our forefathers. The resulting show largely consisted of clowns doing backflips on trampolines while singing about the sovereign colony of Virginia. When Mr. McD came to Orion, he was still trying to live down the resulting scandal.

For our spring show, he chose *Marat/Sade*. If you've never heard of the play, it might help to know that the full title is: *The Persecution and Assassination of Jean-Paul Marat as Performed by the Inmates of the Asylum of Charenton under the Direction of the Marquis de Sade.*

A far cry from munchkins and flying monkeys, wouldn't you say?

The show was amazing. I have never seen a production like it on a high school stage. I only played a background lunatic, but there were times even I forgot we were onstage. I was so lost in everyone's performances, I actually believed we were in an insane asylum. It was *that* frighteningly real.

You can imagine how the parents reacted. Seeing their little darlings writhing onstage as inmates of an asylum. There was outrage over the raw nature of the production. Not to mention the underlying message of class struggle that more than a few of our Fortune 500 parents took personally. But mainly everyone was upset over the fact that *Marat/Sade* wasn't a musical.

The Orion Academy Spring Theatrical Production is *always* a musical.

Mr. McD was forced out of Malibu in disgrace . . . *and* with a three-picture deal from Warner Bros. It's amazing how often scandal leads to success out here in La-La Land. So, while

Mr. McD is prepping the film version of the David Mamet children's play *The Revenge of the Space Pandas*, we're left behind to deal with the *Marat/Sade* repercussions for this year's musical.

Repercussion #1: At the beginning of the year, Headmaster Collins handed Mr. Randall a list of musicals that no one could have a problem with. It was a very short list, highlighted with *The Sound of Music* and *Oklahoma!* All very good plays, but the kind of stuff we did in the third grade.

From that list Mr. Randall picked *Wizard* because it didn't include Nazis or focus too much on a Red State. Therefore— he explained to a few select students—it would be the least offensive choice to the surrounding community of liberal Hollywood elite.

Okay, there was Tasha Valentine's Wiccan parents who took issue with the stereotypical portrayal of witches. But everyone knows the Valentines only follow Wicca because it's trendier than Scientology this year. Making a stink about the Wicked Witch just makes them seem all the more *out there*.

Which is my very long way of explaining the choice of play. But not why there were four girls onstage.

That requires even more exposition.

Little Women,
The Musical

"Okay, Heather, find the light," Mr. Randall said to Dorothy #3. She was standing on the edge of the wash from the spotlight.

"But I'm *in* the light," Heather said with her customary deep sigh of exasperation (aka The Sigh That Launched a Thousand Fits). Heather's sighs are so impressive that I'm constantly surprised she doesn't drop from lack of oxygen by the time she's done letting them out.

Now, while it was true that the light from the spot was in the general area of the stage where Heather was standing, she wasn't technically *in* it. Mr. Randall had Jimmy, the stage manager, focus the spotlight like that on purpose. Half the cast still didn't notice when they were standing in total shadow onstage.

"You're close," Mr. Randall said with a diplomacy that comes from years of experience. "But you need to be in the hot spot, where the light is brightest. So please, Heather, find the light."

"It's a *spotlight*," Heather insisted. "It moves wherever the person behind it points the thing. Shouldn't the light find me?"

"Technically, that's true," Mr. Randall said with continued diplomacy. "But you need to know this for all the lighting instruments. You're not always going to be in the spotlight, Heather."

I'm sure Heather would disagree.

Heather gave another sigh that could be heard back in the cheap seats. She then moved a small step stage left and stopped.

"That's closer," Mr. Randall said.

"Here, lighty, lighty, lighty," I whispered softly.

I guess it wasn't soft enough because Mr. Randall shot me a look from his seat one row in front of me.

I shrugged my apology and focused back on the lost Dorothy.

Your typical spoiled Hollywood brat, Heather Mayflower used to go around telling everyone that her family actually owned the original ship that the pilgrims came over on. That is, until back in middle school when poor, clueless Mrs. Sharpe—who was rather dull when it came to understanding a social order wherein thirteen-year-olds were more powerful than teachers—made "the Mayflower Mistake." She mentioned in class that "Mayflower" was actually a common name for boats around that time in history.

Mrs. Sharpe didn't last the full school year.

"Is this better?" Heather asked with a huff.

"Yes," Mr. Randall said. I was the only one who heard him add, "Close enough."

Heather isn't the talented Mayflower in the family. That's her sister, Holly. The younger Mayflower has been working the commercial route for years, has an agent, and has already booked small roles on *Gilmore Girls* and two of the *CSIs*.

In March, Holly had been cast as one of the lead kids in the pilot for a family sitcom that filmed in April. Rumor had it the show was a good bet to be picked up for the next season. We'd all find out the next week. Because of scheduling conflicts with her burgeoning TV career, Holly wasn't free to do the school play this year. And with Holly out of the picture, all it took was one phone call from Daddy to get Heather cast.

I mean . . . her stellar audition cinched the role for her.

Riiiight.

"Jimmy, put the light on Cindy!" Mr. Randall called out to the spotlight operator-stage manager-all around tech maven.

"Cynthia," Cindy quickly corrected.

I stifled a laugh and Mr. Randall stifled his own exasperated sigh as the light hit Dorothy #2, the stunningly beautiful, semiprofessional model *Cynthia* Lakeside.

Which brings us to repercussion #2.

With four Dorothys (or is it Dorothies?), you'd think that would indicate we had four different performances, right? One Dorothy per show. Or maybe we were simply well-stocked in the understudy department?

No. That would make too much sense.

To explain, we need to go back a bit in history. Stick with me now. I had to learn all this for school. I figure this is probably the only place I'm ever going to be able to use this information in my lifetime.

And now we shall enter the Wayback Machine for a brief history of Orion Academy. . . .

The Orion Institute for Astronomical Studies was originally built as a scientific college back in the 1930s. As the name indicates, the college focused solely on the study of astronomy. I think they even found a couple new stars or something. The school's founder, Lewald Merryweather, was one of the foremost scientists in the field. Considering his interest in Hollywood stars rivaled his work studying the stars in the sky, it wasn't surprising that he wanted to set up shop near what was quickly becoming the entertainment capital of the world.

After about two decades of intensive study of both kinds of celestial bodies, Mr. Merryweather was caught in the kind of Hollywood scandal that the current school administration prefers to gloss over during our history lessons. Let's just say it gives new meaning to the big bang theory and leave it at that. As a result, Mr. Merryweather was forced out of the college he had created and run out of town faster than the speed of light.

The college managed to stay in business for another decade until funding eventually dried up. The school and observatory were closed and abandoned. Since nobody likes the look of vacant property—especially in a ritzy beach community—a bunch of parents got together in the early seventies and formed a private high school to make use of the space. In tribute to the original school, they decided to keep the name. Thus, Orion Academy was born.

During those many, *many* decades the college and high school were already in existence, a residential neighborhood grew up around the campus. And now, today, the fine residents along Breakwater Lane don't like all the traffic going through their winding road at night. After an agreement with the neighbors, Orion Academy is now only allowed to have a dozen nighttime events per school year.

Even though everyone freely admits we were here first.

After parents' nights, stargazing nights (we are still called "Orion" Academy for a reason), and other events, that leaves one night of one-acts in the fall and two nights for the spring show. With our growing theater reputation, our shows sell out faster than tickets to the Super Bowl.

Traditionally, our spring show is double cast. The juniors and freshmen perform on Friday night, and the seniors and sophomores perform the same show on Saturday night. But this year, due to an unfortunate aligning of the stars (literally), we were forced into an extra stargazing night, which meant we had to cut one of our shows.

This wouldn't really be a huge problem except that while in the *Marat/Sade* tailspin, the headmaster also buckled under parental pressure over the fear that little Hilary and Bryce might not get a part in the show and decreed that every student who tried out would get "a role of substance."

Translation: No one was going to be Tree #3.

Granted, Trees #1 and #2 are fairly substantial parts in this play—what with the whole apple-picking scene. But Tree #3 just kind of stands around. No lines at all. And it is *far* better to have a stage full of Dorothys, Scarecrows, and Wizards than to have even *one* student with a nonspeaking role.

As a result, we had four Dorothys: two seniors, two juniors. And one performance.

"Cynthia, did you happen to . . . I don't know . . . maybe . . . *alter* your costume ever so slightly?" Mr. Randall asked.

If you ask me, it was fairly obvious she had taken a pair of hedge clippers to the thing. It had about one quarter of the material as the other costumes. Breasts were bursting out on the top, and panties were peeking out on the bottom. And it was all centered around a considerably bare midriff. She was, by far, the sluttiest-looking imitation Kansas farm girl I'd ever seen.

Not that I'd seen many Kansas farm girls in my life.

"What?" Cindy asked with well-practiced innocence. "I thought it would be good if we all looked a little different. So we can stand out some."

Yes, she looked a little different, all right. And, yes, parts of her were standing out, too.

"Somehow, I don't think the audience is going to confuse you girls with one another," Mr. Randall said. He wasn't kidding either. We had quite the selection of Dorothys.

Cindy wasn't the only one who had made some alterations to her costume. Or, more likely, who'd had the maid do some alterations. Three of the four Dorothys had taken a new approach to the familiar outfit. Cindy's modifications were just the most . . . *prominent?*

The aforementioned Heather was wearing a slinky silk

number. Certainly not something any Kansas farm girl would wear to slop the pigs.

The costume award, however, had to go to Suze Finberg, Dorothy #4. Suze chose to add rather than subtract, starting with fringe on the bottom of the dress and capping it off with some crazy beadwork around the neckline. She probably did it herself because she's all kinds of crafty. I figure someday she'll have her own clothing line and maybe even be a guest judge on *Project Runway*.

Once the spotlight moved onto Suze, the beadwork really popped in the light. It sparkled as much as the ruby slippers, but still managed to look subdued so that Suze wasn't overwhelmed by the outfit. It was an amazing balancing act. Not quite appropriate for a farm girl living in the dust bowl, but with this show, we had all given up on appropriate long ago.

Besides, I knew Suze didn't really care about the play. She hasn't liked being onstage since our kindergarten production of *Babes in Toyland*. And yet, there she was. One of the four leads that most of the girls in the show would have killed for.

At this point, you're probably noticing most of us have a history. Ultraexclusive schools tend to feed into one another. With the exception of unexpected bankruptcies and/or being forced to flee Malibu in disgrace, most of my classmates have been through the same educational track starting at Adamson Elementary School, moving on to Pacifica Middle School, and ending where we are currently: Orion Academy.

Every now and then we get a new kid who is seamlessly absorbed into the status quo. On exceedingly rare occasions we get a standout like Dorothy #1: Sam—don't *ever* call her Samantha—Lawson.

Sam blew into the school last year like a Kansas twister and immediately made herself known as a force to be reckoned with in the drama department. And in my life as well.

Sam is the most talented actress-singer-dancer-mime at Orion Academy. Actually, I'm fairly certain that she's the only certified mime on the school roster. She trained with a world-famous mime for a summer during elementary school. Not that I'd ever heard of this "world-famous mime" before she told me about him.

You're probably wondering what it is about all these hyphens I'm using to describe people. For people living in the L.A. area, life is all about the hyphenates. It's how we rate levels of success. I think it all started back when some singers wanted to start acting and actors decided they were singers. That evolved into actor-producers, singer-songwriters, and writer-directors. Nowadays, it's quite commonplace to see business cards that list a person's job title as body double-dog walker.

A triple hyphenate, Sam would easily have been the lone Dorothy for the junior production any normal year. Her costume was the least altered of the bunch. She prefers to use her actual talent to make herself stand out.

Before she started here, Sam went to school in Santa Monica—a nice but not nearly as pricey area south of Malibu. Sam doesn't exactly come from "the other side of the tracks," but we are talking two slightly different childhoods. The tooth fairy used to leave a dollar under her pillow. I always found stock options under mine.

To this day, I don't have a clue what a stock option is.

Sam's only here because her mom teaches English at Orion. They can afford the tuition thanks to some money her grandparents left her, combined with the discount teachers get for their kids to attend. Sam's the only teacher's kid to go to the school. The discount really isn't that much of a discount if you don't have an inheritance to back it up.

"Is it time for my close-up?" Sam asked as she expertly stepped into the hot spot of the light. "Because, I'm ready for it, you know."

"Yes, Ms. Desmond," Mr. Randall said with a wry smile. "How very *Sunset Boulevard* of you."

Sam clasped her right hand to her heart while reaching out to the spotlight with her left. "What light through yonder window breaks?"

"That's the guy's part," I yelled out.

She shot me a look that told me I would later be receiving a lecture on modern gender roles in theater. Then she changed character. "I would like to dedicate this performance to all the little people out there."

"Who are you calling little?" I called to her. "I'm, like, a whole foot taller than you."

"You look to me like a munchkin from up here," Sam shot back with a laugh.

"Are you two quite finished?" Mr. Randall asked. "Because I'd like to get this over with today."

"Sorry," we both muttered.

Now, you might be wondering what I—a guy—was doing at this costume fitting for the four Dorothys.

The reason I gave Mr. Randall was that I wanted to photograph the costumes for the yearbook. But, honestly, I just had nothing better to do.

There was a soccer game going on at the same time, and *everyone* in school was there. It was the reason we weren't having an actual rehearsal even though we sorely needed it with only a week to go before the show.

Everything at Orion Academy shuts down when there's a soccer game. The entire student body makes its way to the soccer field. Even the teachers—who usually can't wait to get out of here on a Friday afternoon—stick around. But with the show only a week away, Mr. Randall needed to fit in the fitting.

Hence my excuse for the photo op. I'll find almost any reason to miss a soccer game. Besides, I was there because I'm friends with Dorothy #1. Best friends, in fact.

Sam is the Dorothy to my Scarecrow . . . the Sandy to my Frenchy . . . and the other half of my vampire pact.

Vampire pact? you ask.

Sam and I have solemnly sworn to each other that if either of us is ever turned into a vampire, the first thing we'll do is turn the other one. What better way to spend eternity than with your best friend? If we had to be tortured souls like in some Anne Rice novel, there's no one else in the world I'd rather share that bleak future with. Besides, wouldn't it be totally cool to have supernatural powers? Extreme strength? Powerful night vision? Able to leap onto second-floor garden balconies in a single bound?

We've also sworn to use the powers for good. We'd only drain the life from criminals or terrorists or people who talk in movie theaters.

More than a fair trade for an immortally tortured soul, if you ask me.

"I think we're good," Mr. Randall said, really stretching the definition of "good," as far as I'm concerned. "You can all get to the—"

"Heads!" Jimmy screamed from the back of the auditorium.

All heads looked up to see a metal lighting instrument dropping from above. It was falling toward the stage—and the Dorothys—below.

The Boy from Oz

I could swear the lighting instrument was falling at seventy-six frames per second. (*Aside:* That's movie talk for slow motion.) And yet, there was nothing anyone could do to stop it.

The speed of the world around me slammed back to normal as the lighting instrument crashed onto the stage only a few small feet from Sam's small feet.

Then there was silence.

That lasted about three seconds. Then the screeching began. First Heather, then Cindy (I mean, Cynthia), and finally Suze.

I'm proud to say that Sam did not get all screechy. She simply stared down at the twisted metal and glass shards that settled around her red-sequined shoes.

"Is everyone okay?" Mr. Randall asked as he bolted out of his seat.

"I think I found the light," Sam replied as she pointed down to the shattered glass and twisted metal.

Leave it to Sam to break the dramatic tension.

Almost.

Jimmy raced past me and leaped onto the stage before Mr. Randall could even get out of his row. When properly motivated, that kid can *move*.

Jimmy is our passive-obsessive stage manager. He can usually be found buzzing around behind the cast and crew, looking over their shoulders to make sure everything meets with his detail-oriented eye. He never quite criticizes anyone directly, but you can always tell when he wants to get in there and do things his way. That's just on a normal day. During emergencies like these—or on opening night—there's no metaphor created that can properly describe his frantic behavior.

Me? I was still at my seat. But I wasn't exactly doing nothing.

Once it was clear that Sam's wit had survived the accident, I started snapping pictures of the aftermath with my trusty digital camera. Not only would the near disaster make front-page news for the school paper, *The Orion Star*, but the shots of the Dorothys freaking out would provide hours of entertainment for Sam and me.

"Okay, Bryan. You've got more than enough pictures for the lawsuits," Mr. Randall said as he gently pushed my camera down. (I hadn't even thought of that!) "Besides, the lighting instrument landed on the *other* side of the stage."

I saw that Mr. Randall's look of concern had been replaced by that same wry smile I so rarely see from other teachers. He must have realized that my camera was aimed at Heather, who was cowering behind the stage-right curtain. She looked like she was afraid the lighting instrument was going to jump up and bite her.

(*Aside:* We rarely refer to lighting instruments as "lights." Technically they're called "lamps." But I didn't want you thinking I was talking about some cheap, plastic desk accessory from IKEA. These things have heft.)

Once the dust settled, Mr. Randall joined Jimmy and the Dorothys up onstage to examine the fallen lamp. As there was nothing I could do but add a well-timed quip, I sat back in my seat. Sam already had the quip quotient quite covered. (Say that five times fast, I dare you.)

"I'm guessing the fitting is over?" Sam asked. "I'd say it was a smashing success."

We both groaned over that one.

"Yes, Sam," Mr. Randall said. "You can all change out of your costumes and get over to the soccer game."

"Thanks," Sam said as she fled the stage, quickly followed by the other Dorothys.

Not that Sam had any intention of going to the soccer game. We aren't big on hanging out with the masses who flock like sheep to the soccer field. We are very much our own people, with lives full of excitement way more interesting than some high school sporting event.

Even though we didn't have any other plans for that particular afternoon, we'd come up with something eventually.

With the shrieking Dorothys gone, I decided to hop up onstage myself and check things out. That's the kind of thing menfolk do, you know. While the girls are off changing out-fits, the guys stand around examining the broken equipment, trying to determine what caused the accident.

Maybe we'd even call in the Malibu CSI team.

"So, what do we think happened here, fellas?" I said as I moseyed up to Jimmy and Mr. Randall. I would have spit some tobacco into a spittoon had either been available.

Actually . . . no, I wouldn't.

"I think that, maybe, the clamp could've rusted through," Jimmy said, pointing to the metal clamp that usually hooked around the pipe grid up above. "I mean, obviously, it rusted through . . . see all the rust . . . and the *through*."

Jimmy doesn't always make the most sense when he speaks. But he was right about the rust. The metal was brown and holey and missing the all-important top part that hooked it to the pipe. (That's about as technical as my terminology is going to get here.)

"I keep telling the headmaster we need to replace this equipment," Mr. Randall said, shaking his head. Suddenly, I had a stellar idea. I'd ask my parents to make a contribution. The Bryan Stark Light Grid has a nice ring to it.

Or, maybe not.

"What about the safety line?" I asked. Each lamp is sup-posed to be clamped tightly to the pipe. But in case some-thing goes wrong, an aircraft cable is looped around the bar to make sure if the clamp goes, something like this doesn't happen.

Jimmy was silent. This in itself was an amazing feat. Jimmy

is never silent. Not even backstage during a performance. Even his whispers are loud and agitated.

"Jimmy?" Mr. Randall asked.

"I can't . . . umm . . . I could've . . . ," Jimmy said. "I mean . . . I might . . ."

It was clear to me that Jimmy didn't want to admit that he could have missed attaching one of the cables. He tends to freak over little mistakes like that. Though, in this case, I guess it wasn't a *little* mistake.

"I'm sorry, Mr. Randall," Jimmy said. "I should have paid more attention. You're always telling me not to rush so much. And I usually listen. I *try* to listen. But there's just—"

"It's okay, Jimmy," Mr. Randall interjected, laying a calming hand on Jimmy's shoulder. I was glad that Mr. Randall stopped him because it looked like Jimmy was on the verge of breaking into tears.

Jimmy is equal parts sweet and intense, with a small dash of scattered in the mix. In spite of that, there's no one else I'd want to have in charge on show night because when he's *on*, he's on *fire*. Unfortunately, the flip side is also true: When he screws up, it tends to be noticeable. Still, he's loyal like a Labrador, doesn't have a mean bone in his body, and is kind of adorkable in his own way.

While Jimmy and Mr. Randall cleaned up the mess, I grabbed a seat in the front row to wait for Sam. It really wasn't a three-person job. I'd probably get in the way.

Besides, I'm incredibly lazy.

I just realized I've been babbling for quite a few pages now.

I never really introduced myself, you know, *properly*. This is the problem with not being a main character. You tend to get lost in the introductions, even when you're the one doing them.

So . . . who am I, anyway?

As I wrote earlier, my name is Bryan Stark. I can't be sure, but I think my last name should be longer. My dad changed it, either for business reasons or because we're in the Witness Protection Program. I honestly couldn't tell you. I think the full last name was something like Starkinovichskysteinenberger . . . or something like that. Though I guess if we were in the Witness Protection Program, he wouldn't have just shortened the name. He would have changed it entirely, to something like Smith or Jones or someone else who starred in *Men in Black*.

I think I may be Jewish, too.

At least, part Jewish. I don't really know much about my dad's family. His parents died before I was born, and I guess he was an only child. I know my mom used to go to some church. I'm not sure which one. We do celebrate Christmas every year, though.

Let's stick with what I do know about myself.

I'm on the periphery of popularity in a school with no losers, slackers, or geeks, but a ton of Future Media Moguls of America. I'm surprisingly grounded (if I do say so myself) considering that I've rarely been lacking for anything in my life. Not that I'm spoiled like those brats on *Laguna Beach*, but I've never had to worry about my college fund.

I haven't quite figured out my hyphenate quotient yet. If pressed, I'd say I'm an actor-photographer. But photography is really more of a pastime than a lifestyle. Let's just say I'm half-a-hyphenate on a quest to complete myself.

Oh, I like that.

I've been acting pretty much for as long as I can remember. I blame my grandma Millie for that. She used to be a Radio City Music Hall Rockette and had small parts in a bunch of Broadway shows in the fifties. I doubt you would have heard of her, but she was scandalous at a time when scandal wasn't nearly as commonplace as it is today. Since I started going to school I've been in at least one play a year. I kind of take after Grandma Millie since I haven't really broken out with any major roles yet myself, but I'm getting there.

Wizard is my first leading role. I play Scarecrow #2. Figures the first time I get a good part I have to share it with someone else.

As for how I look . . . picture if Brad Pitt and Colin Farrell had a love child. That child would look absolutely nothing like me. But it's fun to imagine, isn't it?

Me? I'm kind of tall and kind of skinny. *Lanky*, might be a good word to use. Not by me, mind you. I'd never call myself that, but other people have. They were all born before 1950, but it's been said.

I tend toward a paler shade of pale, which is somewhat annoying because I do live in the beach community of Malibu. What can I say? Credit my father's Eastern European skin tones. Having jet-black hair only makes me look paler than I really am, too. Even my eyes are gray.

Grandma Millie says I look like a young Cary Grant.

Sometimes I wonder if she means that I look like I belong in a black-and-white movie. She's always talking about how handsome ol' C. G. was back in his early movies from the thirties, like *Sylvia Scarlett*.

You ask me? I think I look more like Cary Grant as he is today: dead for over two decades.

But that's only my opinion.

(*Aside:* *Sylvia Scarlett* is not a particularly great film, but it was the first time Cary teamed with Katharine Hepburn, which makes it interesting from a historical perspective alone. In the movie, Kate dresses up as a boy for reasons defying explanation and falls in love with a man while in her drag king disguise. And the movie came out in 1935!)

By the way, Grandma Millie's the one who usually calls me lanky. I'm pretty sure she means it in the kindest way possible.

I could go on about myself but, believe it or not, I'm not my favorite subject. Okay. Don't believe it. But, in all honesty, this story isn't really about me anyway. Think of me as the Greek Chorus. I'm here to comment on the action, but rarely do I get involved.

Okay, I may get *involved*, but I'm not the star. That would be Sam. And though you might think that the story began when the lamp fell, you'd be wrong. As far as I'm concerned, the real inciting action occurred when Sam came back from the dressing room, held her hand out to me like a proper English gentleman, and uttered the following line:

"Shall we go to the game?"

After the Fall

"The *soccer* game?" I asked for the sake of clarity.

"No. *The Pajama Game*," she said, taking full aim with sarcasm.

"Cool! Will there be pillow fights?"

"Come on, it'll be fun."

"Fun? *Really?* And how are we defining 'fun' nowadays, 'cause I'm not seeing it."

Sam gave a Heather-worthy sigh and plopped down in the seat beside me. She looked at me with exasperation that matched her sigh. Like I was the one who had suddenly gone all crazy high schooler, like Kim McAfee in *Bye Bye Birdie*.

We *never* went to the soccer games. It was our thing: total apathy toward all school sporting events.

We watched as the other Dorothys came back from the dressing room. Heather and Cindy were walking together, chatting about something and nothing at the same time. They pretty much ignored us as they made their way up the aisle. The two naturally unnatural blondes were both dressed in a collection of designer names and logos that I won't even bother to list here.

As for my clothes, there was nary a logo in sight. I had on a pair of black vintage jeans and a nondescript T, covered by a midnight blue button-down shirt (untucked, naturally). I'm sure each of these items has a name of some kind on them, but I really don't look for that when I do my shopping. I'm mainly focused on clothing that doesn't emphasize my lack of musculature.

I do know that my shoes were Skechers. But that's because I only have one pair of those. The company tends to make shoes with really thick soles that usually add an inch to my already tall stature, so it's rare that I buy them.

And, okay, the underwear was Calvin Klein, but we all have to pamper ourselves sometimes.

I topped off the look with my grandpop's black fedora. The hat is true vintage and in pretty good shape considering it's way older than me. I wear it as much as I can. Not because it's a statement or anything, I just like it.

While I'm at it, Sam was wearing a designer label–free, cream-colored peasant top, no-name jeans, and comfortably worn sandals. In the small patch of skin at the base of her neck rested a small silver unicorn hanging on a chain.

I can't speak for her underwear. And I wouldn't even if I could.

The last of the Dorothys, Suze, exited the dressing room

in some name-brand jeans with a silver scarf tied around her waist like a belt. She also wore a blue blazer that she had added silver piping to for effect. Given that the school colors are blue and silver, we didn't have to ask what she was dressed for.

Suze paused for a second to look at the remains of the lamp before heading out with a "See you at the game" directed toward Sam and me.

Which was weird, because *everyone* knew we never went to the games.

"It's not like you don't go to rugby games all the time on weekends," Sam said.

"That's different," I said. And it was. The rugby games I go to are played by adults with a love of the game, not high school kids looking to prove their freakishly active brand of superiority.

Not that I'm bitter, or anything.

And don't think it has anything to do with the fact that I'm a spaz on the field . . . any field. Soccer. Football. Baseball. Badminton. You name the game and I've made a complete and utter fool of myself trying to play it. But my refusal to go to a high school game was for a totally different reason. Well, *mostly* different.

"When did you turn into one of the sheep?" I asked.

"It's not sheeplike to go to one game," Sam insisted. "Besides, Hope doesn't miss a game. You don't call her a sheep."

"Extenuating circumstances," I replied, in reference to our other best friend, Hope Rivera. "Besides, I've got *other* issues with her over that."

"You have so many issues that I sometimes lose track."

"It's part of my charm."

But Sam wasn't buying it.

"Are you coming or not?" Sam asked as she stood up. "Because I will go without you."

"And who are you going to sit with and make fun of people?" I asked as I reluctantly stood too.

"Hope," she said with a look of satisfaction.

"She's not half as vicious as I am."

"True," Sam said. "So, you're coming?"

"Like I have a choice?"

"I like to at least give you the illusion."

Together, we left Hall Hall, dropped our books off at our lockers—which are conveniently across from each other— and headed out the school's back exit.

Even though I've lived in Malibu all my life, it's still amazing to push open a set of doors and be greeted by a view of the Pacific Ocean stretching out into forever. I could stare at the endless blue endlessly, and have spent more than a few afternoons lost in the waves. If only this could be one of those afternoons.

The cruelest part of the design for our school is that none of the classrooms actually face out to the ocean. Instead, all the hallways open up to this amazing vista. That student of Frank Lloyd Wright's must have really believed in form following function. Even when this was a scientific college, he knew that the students would spend half their classes staring out at the waves if they could.

Sam slipped off her sandals once we hit the dirt path off the courtyard. She prefers to go barefoot whenever possible. I can't imagine it was comfortable for the short hike past the parking lot and the observatory.

"Are we doing anything this weekend?" Sam asked as we made out way through the trees beyond the observatory. Our campus would be a lot smaller if it weren't for the fact that there was a small forest in between the main campus and the sports fields.

"You want to come work at the store?" I asked. "Mom guilted me into helping with inventory."

Sam was kind enough to act like she was considering before she said, "No thanks."

I couldn't blame her. It's not that I am embarrassed about my mom's job, but it isn't something I go around bragging about either. My mom owns a boutique on Melrose Avenue called Kaye 9. And if you can't guess by the cute name, she's in the business of designing and selling doggie duds along with her best friend and business partner, Blaine.

Every six months she cons me into helping inventory her stock of crazy creations like diamond doggles—jewel-encrusted goggles for your pooch. I've yet to figure out why any dog would need glasses. They aren't even prescription.

"Let me guess," Sam said. "While you and Mom are doing inventory, Dad is off to Colombia for a major drug score."

"No," I said. "Syria for an arms deal."

"I was close."

My dad's job is somewhat less eccentric than my mom's. In

fact, it's so boring that I don't really know for sure what he does. Since he's always traveling the globe for work, Sam and I like to make up wild stories about what his true work is, such as him being an international arms dealer or the head of a major drug cartel.

In reality, he's probably just bringing democratic office supplies to China.

We don't much talk about Sam's father since he up and left her and her mom back when Sam was five. She hasn't heard from him since.

"And you?" I asked as the trees started to open up ahead of us.

"Study, study, study," she replied.

I should have figured. Sam is in constant struggle with her grades. The girl can learn all of her lines for a role in a matter of hours, but has the hardest time with memorizing things for tests. Her grades are good enough—mostly B's and maybe a C or two—but that won't win her a scholarship. She's going to need some kind of help paying for college since her inheritance went for Orion.

As we reached the clearing, a rousing cheer came up from the crowd watching the soccer game.

"For me?" Sam asked demurely as if anyone in the student body had actually been aware of our arrival. "Oh, that's so . . . I'm speechless."

"That's a first," I said, looking out over the Charles E. Martin Bleachers. Yes, our soccer field has bleachers. I told you we take the sport seriously here. "How are we ever going to find Hope in all this?"

"She should be sitting on the end," Sam said, heading us around the field.

"BAAAA!" I said in my best, and loudest, sheep imitation.

She ignored me and tromped over to the stands in her bare feet.

What could I do? I followed.

Baaaaa.

The soccer field is in the middle of a huge clearing in the trees. Two sets of bleachers line either side. The fans from St. James Academy were sitting in the shoddier, metal bleachers, while our fans had the permanent stands built into raised concrete. Between the trees and the opposing stands I wouldn't even be able to stare out at the ocean during the game. I was going to have to watch it.

Fortunately—or unfortunately, depending on how you look at it—Hope was easy to find. She kind of stood out at the end of the second row, dressed all in black, from the bottom of her steel-toe boots to the top of her black beret. A huge plastic purple flower was pinned to the hat. This is pretty much how she looks everyday: all in black, with a burst of color somewhere on her body. She calls the look Goth-Ick.

The only other color that Hope displayed was her amazingly violet eyes. They were contacts, but still pretty cool.

Everything about Hope is pretty cool, in my opinion. She's a writer-actress-free spirit-. As you can see, she's kind of a double-triple hyphenate. I leave her an extra hyphen at the end because she can be anything else she wants to be on any given day.

As if to mock my paleness, Hope has this incredible light brown skin that looks great with her short black hair. Her secondary hyphenate, if you will, is that she's half-Mexican-American and half-California-Blonde (although the California-Blonde part is more a recessive gene).

Hope was quite pointedly sitting on the opposite side of the bleachers from her full California Blonde stepsisters, Anorexia and Bulimia . . . I mean, Alexis and Belinda. Hope's father married their mother about six years ago, and their daughters have been on opposite ends of the bleachers ever since.

"The girls and I saved you seats," Hope said with barely a glance from her notebook. She picked up her bags to clear two seats for us on the bleachers beside her. Maybe it's my suspicious nature, but the fact that she had saved seats made me think that maybe Sam's decision to go to the game wasn't all that spontaneous.

By the way, the "girls" Hope referred to weren't other friends of ours or her long-distance step-sisters. They were Hope's breasts.

Back in middle school, Hope was among the first to develop. We're hoping she's finally stopped. Her chest has become quite formidable. She's always sure to mention the girls as much as possible, if only to beat everyone else to the punch line.

"What's the score?" Sam asked as she slid in next to Hope.

"Score?" Hope asked, still not looking up.

"Of the game?"

"Game?" Hope questioned.

"Never mind," Sam said as she tapped Jason MacMillan on the shoulder in front of her.

"Tied, four–four," Jason replied without taking his eyes off the game. His right arm was locked with his girlfriend, Wren Deslandes.

"Hey, Scarecrow," I said to Jason.

"Hey, Scarecrow," he answered back.

He and I were Scarecrows #1 and #2 respectively. As it so happened, Hope and Wren were Glindas #1 and #2.

"Go, Comets," I deadpanned as I sat. "Rah."

Hope shot me a playful grin behind Sam's back. Even though Hope was busy writing, I knew her head was totally in the game too. Considering her on-again–off-again-boyfriend, Drew Campbell, was one of the players, she wouldn't miss a second of the action. Though I doubt she wanted it to look that way.

"Never thought I'd see the day," Hope said to me.

"Neither did I," I replied.

Hope has known of my hatred of school sports—especially soccer—for way longer than we've even known Sam. I've actually known Hope almost all my life, but we didn't really become friends until she and Sam became friends. Now I don't know why we didn't hang out together sooner.

A shout reflexively pulled my attention to the field. The ball was getting perilously close to the St. James goal. Everyone on our side jumped up to cheer, except Hope and me. When the goalie caught the ball and sent it in the opposite direction, I felt vindicated for not bothering to move my butt off the bleachers. I'd rather expend the energy on an actual score, if at all.

I saw a look pass from Hope to Sam when she returned to her seat. I was *definitely* out of the loop on something.

Hope caught me catching her look. "What's a good rhyme for carrion?" she quickly asked.

"Carry on?" I asked. It was hard to hear clearly over the crowd noise.

"No, *carrion*," Hope repeated. "You know, rotting flesh."

"Oh," I said. "How about Marion?"

Hope shook her head and looked at Sam for a more useful suggestion.

"Bulgarian?" Sam guessed, refusing to turn her head away from the game.

"You guys are no help." Hope went back to her notebook. It looked like she was onto something. "Scratch that," she said as she started scribbling. "You did give me an idea."

"Marion the carrion?" I asked. "She used to be librarian."

Hope ignored me as she finished her work.

"How's this?" she asked. *"The darkening moon sets upon the sea, as pain and grief wash over me. My beloved, Daisy, is carrion. With me to only carry on."*

"Brilliant!" I said with more excitement than I had managed to express for the game so far.

"Best you've written in a while," Sam added, holding out both her hands for a double-pumped thumbs-up.

I guess we didn't realize how loud Hope was, because Wren turned to look at the three of us like we were full-on Medea.

(*Aside*: Medea is a character from Greek mythology who goes all crazy and kills her sons to get back at her husband. She has a whole play about her and everything.)

Lest you (like Wren) think we lost all sense of artistic criticism, I assure you Hope is a really amazing writer. *Really*. She's got reams of poetry and prose a billion times better than anything you'd find in your average teen's blog of despair. But Hope only shares those works with the inner circle, namely Sam and me. The journal she was writing the bad verse in is her *Book of the Dead Puppy Poetry, Volume Six*. The book—and its five predecessors—were created back when she was eleven, on the day after Hope's stepmother and two stepsisters moved in . . . and the moving van backed over Hope's cocker spaniel, Daisy.

Hope was understandably devastated. She wrote about it in her journal as any eleven-year-old might do. Naturally she blamed the entire thing on her stepmother for moving in on her and her dad. The next day, Hope's private journal somehow came up during a session with her therapist. That was when Hope realized that her private writings were no longer her own. From that day on, the only writing her family has ever seen her do is to lament the passing of her poor Daisy. You'd be surprised the number of ways she can fit the phrase "pushing up daisies" into a poem.

"Now that that's done," Sam said, "why don't you watch your boyfriend?"

"Please stop referring to him as *my* boyfriend," Hope said politely. "He's got an identity of his own. We do not subscribe to labels. I do not own him. He does not own me."

"Hope, he's got the ball," Sam said. "Cheer."

"Fine," Hope said as she rose from the wooden bench. "GO, DREW! SHOVE IT DOWN THEIR THROATS!"

Such a dainty little darling, isn't she?

Drew must have heard her, because he stumbled slightly. Probably from shock. I doubt she was usually this vocal during a game.

Drew recovered and took the ball downfield. He weaved in and out of his opponents as he made his way toward the goal.

Soon everyone on the Orion Academy side—except me—was on their feet along with Hope screaming encouragement. The noise was way louder than anything I've ever heard from a theater audience.

Yet another reason why I hate sports.

"Go, Drew!" Hope screamed with genuine excitement now. "Come on!"

I was forced to stand to see what was going on. It was a clear shot to the goal. Drew was going to score. I checked the scoreboard. There wasn't much time left in the game. It could be the winning goal.

"Kick it in!" Hope yelled. Her brassy voice carried out over everyone else's in the stands.

Just as it looked like Drew was going to score, a St. James player came out of nowhere and stole the ball away. Drew looked even more shocked than everyone watching.

The Orion fans—except me—let out a collective groan as we all sat back down.

"Well, that yelling clearly served no purpose," Hope said as she opened up her notebook again.

"No, wait," Sam said. "Eric's got the ball."

Oh, great.

Eric Whitman is Drew's best friend and, in my humble opinion, a total asshat. He's also the star of the soccer team and the only junior on the starting roster. And if you must know, he's a soccer stud-surfer boy-class president-blond god-total asshat.

I could build up the suspense here, but I'm not a member of the Eric Whitman fan club, so I'll keep it simple: He took the ball back down the field, scored a goal, and won the game.

Go, Comets.

Blah.

Desire Under the Elms
(Well . . . They Could Have Been Oaks)

Sam unilaterally decided that we would hang with Hope while she waited for Drew to finish up. To be honest, I didn't much mind. Everyone who was leaving the bleachers was heading for the parking lot. If we left with them, it would take, like, a half hour to get out the one exit.

So we waited. While the soccer team shook hands with the guys from St. James. While they went through their cooldown stretches. While they had their on-field, post-game wrap-up.

We weren't the only ones waiting either. The personal fan clubs of the players were also waiting. Sam, Hope, and I sent a few silent glances back and forth as we watched Heather Mayflower standing on the sidelines. She was waiting for her boyfriend, Jax, to get off the field. Even in the open air, her award-winning sighs were audible.

Sam's mom was at the game too. She was sitting in the

middle of the stands with the faculty contingent. I doubt they were waiting for any of the players on the field. They were probably sticking around until the parking lot cleared too.

We would have gone over to say hi, but we prefer to treat Sam's mom like a teacher as much as possible while we're in school and keep the mingling to a minimum. Even when we're all just sitting around with nothing else to do.

Finally, Coach Zachary dismissed the team.

Jax was the first player to make it to the sideline. He clearly knew better than to keep Heather waiting any longer than necessary.

Before he even had the chance to kiss her hello, Heather was regaling him, and everyone in the vicinity, with the death-defying tale of the falling lamp. This was one of the best performances I'd ever seen from her. It had heart, drama, and actual pathos. Not to mention that it was even more of a fantasy than a play about a wizard, munchkins, and a magical world over the rainbow.

My personal favorite part of the story was when she "valiantly pushed the other Dorothys out of the way, putting [her] own life at risk to save her less talented costars."

I *so* wish I were kidding about that.

"Are you okay?" Hope asked Sam when she heard the story.

Sam let out a derisive snort to let Hope know it was nothing.

In the meantime, I was so busy trying not to overhear Heather's conversation that I totally didn't notice that Drew and Eric were walking right toward us. They were all sweaty and dirty from the match and, quite frankly, not that fun to be around even at their cleanest.

Not that Eric looked bad. Eric *never* looks bad. He's a prime example of the beach blond perfect specimen that you see in every movie set in California since the dawn of color film. You know, the kind who doesn't actually exist in real life, except for the one walking toward us with his sculpted abs, playfully tousled hair, and typical dimples. It was enough to make me want to puke.

And then there's Drew. He's not the textbook pretty boy that Eric is, but that's what makes him even more attractive, in my opinion. Sure, Drew has great, sandy brown hair, a tall, non-lanky body, and incredibly muscular legs. But it's the imperfections that work for him. He's got this little crescent-shaped scar on his chin that he's had since he was eight, a slightly crooked smile, and no dimples whatsoever to speak of. He has what I call "attainable good looks." The boy can definitely turn some heads, but he's not so perfect that he's entirely out of your league.

"Hey, Sunshine," Drew said as he gave Hope a kiss. Even I can appreciate the irony of calling her Sunshine when she wears black almost exclusively.

"Good game," Hope said. "And, you stink."

"Thanks," Drew replied, taking her into a full-on hug that looked more pleasant than it probably smelled.

"Hi," Eric said to Sam.

"Hi," Sam said back.

Sam's toes were digging into the ground. Eric was trying to put his hands in nonexistent pockets.

Me? I guess I disappeared for a moment. Because no one even *bothered to acknowledge my presence!*

"Did you watch the game?" Eric asked, with his eyes glued to Sam.

Considering there was no other reason for us to be at the soccer field, I found it to be a fairly obvious question.

"Caught the end," Sam replied. "Saw you score."

"Yeah," he replied, and actually kicked his foot into the dirt.

I think I may have laughed or snorted or something, because Sam shot me a look. I guess I was kind of staring, too.

"Can I talk to you?" Eric asked, motioning with his head that they should walk away.

"Sure," Sam said a little more eagerly than I thought the question warranted.

Eric led Sam off to the trees. He walked with a confident swagger that, I guess, comes from scoring the winning point at a game that cinched Orion a spot in the finals. Next Friday, while two other teams fought it out for the final spot in the finals, our guys could relax until the actual game in two weeks.

A couple fans high-fived Eric along the way into the woods, but he didn't even slow down to bask in the glory. He and Sam stopped at the edge of the tree line. Even at a distance, their conversation wasn't looking any less awkward than it had when they were standing right next to me.

Since it wasn't like I was going to stand there openly gawking at them, I turned my attention back to Hope and Drew.

That? Was a mistake.

"Did you hear me cheering?" Hope asked.

"Yeah," Drew replied. "Didn't you see me trip?"

"So what? I shouldn't have cheered?"

"No," Drew said. "It just caught me off guard. You've never done that before. You've never taken your head out of that book at a game before."

"No wonder," Hope said. "Considering the kind of appreciation I get."

"What are you talking about?" Drew asked.

"Never mind. I need to talk to Mr. Telasco about something." Hope stormed off to speak to the art teacher.

Leaving Drew and me there alone.

"So," I said.

"So," he said.

Since neither of us had much more to say to each other, I turned my attention back to Sam and Eric. It looked like they were no longer having any trouble coming up with things to talk about. They were smiling and laughing, and her hand was resting on his arm.

"What are they up to?" I asked. Unfortunately, I asked it out loud, and for some reason, Drew thought I was talking to him.

"Who?" he asked.

"Over there." I pointed. "My best friend . . . your best friend. What are they doing?"

"Getting friendly?" Drew said.

"Very funny," I replied.

"Didn't expect to see you here," Drew said.

"Didn't expect to be here," I said.

"What did you think?"

"Of the game?"

"No," Drew said. "Of the new uniforms."

"The blue clashes with your eyes."

"My eyes *are* blue."

"See what I'm saying?"

Drew looked me over with disdain. "Rarely."

He walked away, shaking his head.

His stride didn't have nearly the same swagger as Eric's, yet I couldn't take my eyes off him. Or, more specifically, I couldn't take my eyes off that part of the body where he would swagger if he could. Just above those incredibly muscular legs, those soccer shorts only managed to accentuate Drew's best asset.

Pun fully intended.

In case you haven't figured it out by now, my interest in guys tends toward something other than just friendship. Not that I have many guy friends. But I do have guy *interests*.

This isn't something new. I've kind of suspected it my entire life. It's not like there weren't signs growing up. Certain leanings, as they say. Nothing definite, but definitely something.

Those leanings grew pretty hard to ignore when I was about fourteen.

My growth spurt was more like an explosion. I'm currently six feet tall, and we're not sure I've stopped growing. I started shopping in the men's department early.

Finding clothes has never been a problem for me. I have very specific tastes. I know what I like and what I look good in. That is, anything that camouflages my wiry frame. But shopping trips have always been in and out with an armload of bags in no time flat. That's why I was so surprised when it would take forever to pick out the right underwear. I would just stand there comparing the boxes for boxers, briefs, and boxer-briefs.

Eventually I realized the dilemma: I wasn't nearly as interested in the underwear as I was the pictures of the guys on the packages.

But don't worry. This isn't one of those angst-filled books where I'm struggling to come to terms with what it all means. I've long since accepted it. I'm gay. I'm over it. There will be no endless, teary-eyed, internal dialogues. No tormented, sleepless nights. I am 100 percent at ease with who I am.

Except for the fact that I haven't told anyone yet.

In my defense, none of my friends have announced to me that they are straight. Until they do that, I don't see much point in making some grand declaration of my own. Besides, I've got more important things to worry about.

"Eric asked me out."

"What?" I asked. I think I may have actually done a double take as Eric walked past us toward Drew and Hope.

"Eric asked me out," Sam repeated with something sickeningly close to glee.

"When?"

Sam looked at me like I was the one acting like a fool. "Just now."

"No. When did he want to go out?"

"Oh. Tomorrow."

"And you said no, right?"

For some reason, she looked at me like I was twice the fool. "*No.*"

"He asked you out? For tomorrow night? And you said yes?"

"Now you've got it!"

I gave her a similar "You're the fool" look. "Who asks someone out one day in advance? Couldn't he at least give you *some* notice?"

"Who are you? Miss Manners?"

"At least I *have* manners," I mumbled.

"Oh, my God!" Hope shrieked as she ran up to Sam. "I just heard."

And now, I swear, they both giggled.

Giggled!

I'm sorry, but we do not giggle.

Hope and Sam were acting so girly that I had to tune them out. I still couldn't believe she said yes. It is incredibly rude to ask someone out for the next day. And, if you ask me, it's also a little desperate to accept so quickly. Hadn't Sam ever heard of playing coy? I know we tend to make fun of girls who play coy, but this would be different. This would have been playing coy with a purpose.

"Are you in?" Hope asked me.

"Sorry?" I hadn't heard a word of what they were saying.

"We're going to hit Rodeo tomorrow and find something perfect for Sam to wear," Hope said.

Suddenly we'd gone from being coy to being materialistic. It was quite possible I had stepped into some kind of alternate universe.

"I don't know," Sam said. I suspect she was mentally going over her finances.

By the way, "Hitting Rodeo" is code for shopping the outlets in nearby Camarillo. We don't ever shop on Rodeo Drive in Beverly Hills. First of all, no one around here does. That place is for our parents . . . or tourists. Not to mention that Rodeo Drive is somewhat outside of Sam's budgetary constraints.

"I'm sure I've got something that will be fine," Sam added in a tone that didn't sound certain in the least.

I've seen Sam's entire wardrobe and she has *plenty* of outfits that would be more than fine for a date with Eric Whitman.

"We don't need *fine*," Hope said.

Don't say it, I silently pleaded.

"We need *super*fine."

She said it. And Sam bought it. They were going shopping.

"That's settled," Hope said, then turned to me. "Wanna come?"

"Can't," I said. "I'm going to be busy gouging out my eyes this weekend. But your plans sound almost as fun."

"So I thought," Hope said dismissively. "Hey! We can look for prom dresses!"

"Prom shopping, too? You're just trying to make me jealous," I said.

Now, don't get me wrong. I love to shop. I can't think of a better way to spend the weekend than by hanging out at the mall with my friends. The problem is, my friends are girls. Most of the time this fact doesn't really come into play in our relationship. Sometimes, however, they're *really* girls. And that's the kind of shopping trip they had in mind. All day trying on outfit after outfit to find the most perfect of the perfect, while I wait outside the dressing room for hours, leaning on the racks, trying to stay awake.

I could probably hang out in the dressing rooms with them, but we really prefer to keep that area of our lives separate.

"If you're going shopping for a prom dress, I would like to remind you that I look good in blue, green, and especially gray," I said. "So, those are good colors to match your dress to . . . you know, my vest or tie or whatever."

"Noted," Sam said. "Are you sure you don't want to come?"

I reminded her of my work commitment at my mom's store.

"Then I guess we won't see each other till Monday," Sam said.

I would have reminded her that a weekend has two days in it, but I knew what she meant. We had that history test on Monday. She was planning to spend all day Sunday cramming for it. You'd think we could study for the test together, but Sam's cram sessions are a solitary practice. This is more out of respect for our friendship than anything. The one time we tried to study together, I dared to take a moment to make a snack before we started and she nearly killed me.

Hope and Sam were already busy putting together their game plan for their shopping trip.

"So who needs a ride home?" I asked.

"Drew's going to take me," Hope said.

"I'm waiting for Mom," Sam said.

"Oh," I replied as I realized there was no reason for me to be there at all.

The Suppliants

My weekend was fairly uneventful. I spent most of Saturday at Kaye 9 inventorying stuff like doggie vests, shoes, and lingerie (ew!). I studied a bit for the history test. I didn't even bother trying to call Sam on Sunday since she wouldn't have answered the phone.

Truthfully, that's not the reason I didn't talk to her. I wasn't interested in hearing all about her date with Eric. By the time Monday morning rolled around, I can't say I was any more intrigued about what they did and did not do. Conveniently, with all thoughts on the test first thing in the morning, there was little time for gossip. Which brings us to . . .

Lunch.

It was turning out to be another beautiful Malibu day. There was no need to wear a jacket while eating at the Kenneth Graham Pavilion. That's our version of a lunchroom. It's not so much a room as it is a wooden deck at the north end of the school. The pavilion was built in an octagonal shape with a wood roof that rises to a peak like a circus tent. There are no walls, just beams holding up the roof. Heaters in the ceiling keep us warm on chilly days, and plastic blinds come down on the sides if it's windy and rainy.

Contrary to popular belief, it does rain in Southern California. We just prefer to contain all of our rain to a few months—usually February and March—and spend the rest of the year with dry, sunny skies. But we are by the beach, so it can get chilly on occasion.

Since the pavilion juts out from the main building we have an unobstructed view of the ocean, the observatory, and the courtyard. That beats cinderblock walls painted institutional gray any day.

I grabbed two chicken soft tacos and dropped them onto my tray. Since I wasn't much hungry for anything else, I pulled a fruit juice from the refrigerator and made my way to the pavilion. That is another reason we don't call it a lunchroom. There are no facilities to actually make lunch. No ovens or stoves. Not even a lunch lady or a hairnet. The administration contracts with restaurants in the area to bring in food every day. The school calls it a "catered lunch." I call it pretentious.

If the pavilion were a typical lunchroom in a typical school, this would be the point of the story where some character would discuss the social structure of the lunchroom seating. The character—in this case, me—would direct your attention to the tables with the jocks and cheerleaders, the brains, the arty crowd, the potheads, and the slackers. Then he'd (or I'd) go on to explain how the social groups were strictly defined, rarely mixed with one another, and all that junk.

Yeah, we've got none of that here.

With only two hundred students in the entire school, we have a fair amount of overlap. The jocks are all brains. The potheads, too. We don't *have* any slackers. No cheerleaders either. The only real organized sports we have are boys' soccer, girls' volleyball, and mixed-gender swimming. None of those sports really call for cheerleaders.

Surprisingly, we don't have any cliques of any kind at Orion Academy. We all pretty much hate each other individually and equally. We all *like* each other in much the same way. The pavilion is one big melting pot of friendship, with a large amount of passive aggression stirred in.

Except for my table, that is. Sam, Hope, and I regularly dine at the table reserved for the Drama Geeks. Please note that this is a self-proclaimed title. A badge we wear with pride. We're the outsiders. The ones who don't follow the status quo. You know the type: the people who randomly burst into song in between classes for absolutely no reason whatsoever.

We're the closest thing to an arty crowd around here, except that we are fairly mainstream when it comes to our entertainment choices. None of that overwrought, over-blown, independent film junk. *Unless* it stars a really hot actor trying to break out of his typical big-budget film roles.

Not that I'm talking about Colin Farrell again. I'm just saying.

Sam, Hope, and I make up the regulars at the table. As do Jimmy—who's usually pounding down a few bottled

Frappuccinos—and Tasha, the resident vegan true-Goth chick. (Hope usually runs all of her Goth-Ick looks by Tasha to make sure she's not being offensive to the actual spirit of the movement.)

Otherwise, the rest of the Drama Geeks filter in and out depending on the day. We also have non-drama students pop by the table from time to time, but the less said about them the better.

As I reached the table, the only other people there so far were Sam and Hope.

Today, Hope was sporting a red belt with her all-black outfit, highlighted by these flaming red contacts. She did look a touch demonic. It was especially odd, considering she takes the whole concepts of demons and religion more seriously than most people I know. She refuses to take part in my vampire pact with Sam. Hope subscribes more to the Buffyverse definition of vampires, seeing them as soulless demons only interested in killing. She won't even *consider* the possibility that being a vampire could be all cool and romantically tormented.

She has, however, promised to stake Sam and me if it turns out that she's right and we're wrong. And really, what more can you ask from a friend than for her to kill you to save you from an immortal life as a demonic creature?

"So, how did you do on the test?" Sam asked before I could even sit.

"Failed horribly," I said. "You?"

"Miserably," she replied.

"Oh, shut up," Hope said. "You both did fine like always."

I was pretty sure I did, but I could tell Sam was genuinely doubtful.

"Now that you finally got here," Hope said to me, before turning to Sam, "Sam can tell us all about her date."

I chose not to say anything.

"I knew I wasn't going to get through lunch without the inquisition," Sam said. She may have been protesting, but she was also leaning into the table so no one else could hear but us.

"What's the story, morning glory?" Hope sang as she leaned in to match Sam. She grabbed my sleeve and pulled me forward too, so Sam could start with the storytelling.

I'll save you all the gory details. You can thank me later. Sam and Eric went to dinner at CPK—that's California Pizza Kitchen, for the nonnatives—and then to some movie. Honestly, I wasn't much listening, so I couldn't tell you which movie. Apparently it wasn't worth seeing. I think it starred Ben Affleck.

Anyway, the story on the date itself wasn't important. It was what she said when she finished the story that you need to know.

"If it's okay with you, Bryan."

I have *got* to start listening more when I'm part of a conversation.

"What?" I asked.

"Bryan!" Hope said, smacking me in the shoulder. She does that a lot. For someone with such a sweet disposition (*cough-cough*), she has a nasty left hook.

"Sorry," I said, seeing my excuse walking in this direction. "I was distracted when I saw the matching Abercrombie & Fitch–ness of your *boyfriends* coming this way."

Sam quickly turned in their direction, then, just as quickly, turned back to share a bug-eyed look at Hope. Then, even more quickly, she swung her attention back to me.

I swear all that happened in, like, point-zero-five seconds.

"He's not my boyfriend," Sam said. "But that's kind of what I was just saying. Now don't get mad."

Never a good opening.

"I know we always said we'd go to the prom together if we weren't seeing anyone," Sam said, reminding me of our oft-discussed agreement. "It's not like Eric and I are officially *seeing* each other or anything, but he did ask me."

"To the prom?" I asked as I watched Eric and Drew approach. I swear they were walking in slow motion across the cafeteria. I further swear I heard the "plink-plink" clock-ticking sound from 24 as they walked our way.

That last part could have been purely my imagination.

"Yeah," Sam said. "But I won't go with him if you don't want me to. We did sort of promise each other."

"It wasn't really a *promise*," I said, trying for magnanimous, but probably sounding a bit whiny. Eric and Drew were almost at the table.

"Whatever," Sam said. "Is it okay?"

What was I supposed to say? It *wasn't* okay. Sure, we hadn't technically promised each other we would go to the prom together. But we had been talking about it since forever. Now I was being all rushed to make a decision because asshat Eric was coming to the table.

Oops! Too late. Already here.

Arsenic and Old Lace

"How's it going?" Eric asked as he put his tray down on our table.

Here's the problem with not having well-defined lunch-room cliques: Anyone feels that he can just sit wherever he wants.

Drew came around the table and slid in between Hope and me. He gave her a little kiss on the cheek as he pushed his way in. On the other side of the table, Eric sat beside Sam. Neither one of them seemed too sure if they were supposed to kiss or not. They both settled for some weird shoulder-bump thing that—in my opinion—could not possibly have been what either one had intended.

"And what's the lunchtime topic today?" Drew asked. "Not us, I hope, Hope."

"Not *you*, at least," I said as I took a bite of my chicken soft taco.

"Prom," Hope quickly said.

Sam's eyes about bugged out of her face this time.

"Really?" Eric asked, looking directly at Sam. "And what were you saying about it?"

You know how cartoon characters look the moment they realize they've walked off a cliff and there's nothing beneath their feet but a huge drop? Yeah, Sam looked very much like that. She clearly did not want to get into a discussion about the prom in front of me until we got over the whole "implied promise" thing. At the same time, she didn't want to be totally rude and ignore a direct question from Eric either.

She looked somewhat like her head was about to explode. As her friend, it was my job to come in and save her.

"Um," she faltered. "Well . . . it's like . . ."

Notice I didn't say, "*Rush* in and save her." I felt it wasn't entirely out of line to let her struggle for a bit first. Not to be harsh, but we had gone from total trio to fifth wheel scenario in one weekend. I wasn't about to make this any easier on her.

Okay, maybe I was being a tad harsh.

"Prom!" Sam blurted out as if it answered Eric's question.

At this point, I could bear no more. "Sam told us you guys are going together," I said.

"Did she?" Eric asked, smiling this disgustingly large grin as he looked directly at Sam. "She hasn't told *me* that, yet. All she said was she'd get back to me."

Sam definitely got points for that.

"Well . . ." Sam started to look like she was hanging off that cliff again.

"Wait till you see my dress," Hope jumped in, speaking to Drew and me. "We got it this weekend at this great vintage shop. It's this black—"

"Naturally," Drew and I said in unison. Purely unintentional, I assure you.

This time, Hope smacked Drew, not me.

"Lace Chanel evening dress in a kind of forties couture style with a bolero jacket," Hope continued. "It was originally made for Shelley Winters before she gained all the weight."

I started to say something, but stopped myself. There was no polite way to ask the question. And I didn't want to get smacked again.

"Who's Shelley Winters?" Eric asked.

It was all I could do not to snort with derision. No. That was *not* the question I was afraid to ask.

"You know," Hope said, "the actress from the original *Poseidon Adventure*."

I could see in Eric's eyes that he had no clue what she was talking about. "Nope," I said. "Try again."

"The hillbilly mom from *Pete's Dragon*," Sam tried.

"Disney musicals? Not a chance," I said, turning to Drew. "Your turn."

Drew didn't bother to look at me when he said, "The grandmom on *Roseanne*."

A look of relief washed over the girls' faces as Eric finally got the reference. *Thank God for Nick at Nite.*

"Oh," he said, "but she was—"

"Quite the voluptuous stunner in her younger days," Hope said threateningly.

"Yeah," Drew said, "but even then, she didn't have . . . never mind."

"Go ahead," Hope said threateningly to Drew. "Say it."

"Say what?" Drew asked, taking a bite of his taco, then speaking through his food. "Don't know what you're talking about."

"Can you please not do that?" I asked, wiping a piece of spit chicken off my tray.

Drew held up his hands in what I guess was some lame form of an apology as he chewed his food. Once upon a time, Drew used to have manners. I guess things like that all depend on the company you keep.

Obviously, Drew and I had had the same thought about Shelley Winters and vintage Chanel. I'm glad I wasn't the only one who wondered how they'd both fit in the same dress. Now, don't get me wrong. Shelley Winters was never a stick figure. She came from a time when beautiful women in Hollywood were judged by their curves, not by how many ribs you could see peeking through their dresses. Her body type was originally quite similar to Hope's.

But not entirely.

"What did I miss?" Eric asked.

I didn't see Drew's face, but I could tell it mirrored mine.

Mine was silently saying, "Shut up, idiot."

But Hope saved us both at her own expense. "Okay. Fine. It does have to be let out a bit in certain areas."

"Let out?" Eric asked. "Oh! You mean the chest!"

Drew and I shoved the rest of our tacos in our mouths simultaneously. We were having no part of this.

"Can they even do that with lace?" Eric asked, showing a far better grasp of fashion than I ever thought he would possess.

"I'm sure my mom's people can," Hope said. Her mom, Natalie Ellis, is one of *the* top designers in the fashion world. She has design houses in Los Angeles, New York, and Paris, and her work can regularly be seen on the red carpet at all the major events. Since she has to split her time evenly between the three design houses, Hope lives with her dad and steps.

"But I hate asking them for favors," Hope said. "Alexis and Belinda do it all the time and they're not even *related*. Why do my parents have to get along so well?"

"Bitter divorce is *so* the way to go," I said. Not that I know anything about that subject. My parents are still firmly together. There's nothing bitter about their marriage either. It's hard to work up the bitterness when my father's out of town so much and my mom's too easily distracted by puppies to have any abandonment issues.

"You should ask Suze," Sam said as Dorothy #4 was passing with her tray. "She'd probably listen to what you want more than one of your mom's flunkies."

"That's a great idea," Hope said. "Hey, Suze! Hold on a sec!"

Suze dropped her tray at the next table and came over to ours before Hope could even get up. Suze is one of those girls who bounces around the lunchroom, eating at a different table every day. She is equally friendly with everyone, which makes half the girls in school hate her, naturally.

"What's up?" she asked as she knelt on the end of the bench beside Sam.

"A project," Hope said, with a gleam in her eye. "If you're interested, that is. It's a fashion emergency."

"My favorite kind," Suze said as she slid down to sit on the bench.

Hope pulled her cell phone out of her bag. "Check this out." As she passed it to Suze, I caught a glimpse of a black dress on the screen.

"Hope, we're not supposed to have cell phones in school," Drew needlessly reminded her as he quickly looked around the pavilion. Sometimes he can be incredibly annoying with the worrying. There wasn't a teacher in sight. Not a surprise, really. All the teachers *hate* lunch duty, and usually find some way to be late.

"I'm not using it to call anyone," Hope said.

"Not like she could if she wanted to," I added. One of the problems with having a school built halfway up the side of a mountain is that we have lousy cell phone reception. Even if we were allowed to have them in school, they would be utterly useless.

"I see," Suze said as she scrutinized the image. She reminded me of a doctor examining a patient. That's how intensely she looked at the photo of the dress.

We were all so focused on Suze studying the dress that we didn't notice Jax lumbering up to the table until it was too late.

"Yo, Drew, what's—" As Jax leaned across the table to give Drew five, or bump fists, or whatever it is *some* guys do, he spilled his soda all over Sam's shirt.

"Jax, you idiot!" Eric yelled as he jumped out of his seat. Drew was also up in a flash. I would have jumped up too, but the other guys looked like they had matters well in hand.

"Geez. Sorry," Jax said. His hands were rubbing at the quickly setting stain on Sam's top.

Sam grabbed the moving hands and pushed them off her. "It's all right," she said through clenched teeth. Honestly, she was handling it far better than I thought she would. Though, that could have something to do with the fact that as soon as Eric yelled out, the entire pavilion had gone quiet. Everyone was looking at our table.

"You'll want to put some vinegar and water on that," Suze suggested.

"I'll be right back," Sam mumbled as she left the pavilion. She was in such a rush that she left her sandals under the table and ran out in her bare feet.

I couldn't help but notice that all heads were turning to follow her. I was really annoyed to see Jax's girlfriend looking like she was enjoying the whole thing. But that's Heather Mayflower for you. She specializes in taking pleasure in other people's pain.

"Idiot!" Eric said again.

"Dude, I said, *sorry*," Jax said as he moved off to join his girlfriend.

While Eric and Suze wiped the remaining soda from the

table, I continued to watch Jax and Heather. The kiss she gave her boyfriend made me suspect that the accident wasn't so much of an accident. What a petty little Dorothy she could be.

Heather was totally jealous that Sam got to sing "Over the Rainbow." Cynthia was too, but she at least acted like it didn't bother her. It didn't help that Sam is a junior. All the seniors in the play thought the best number should go to a senior. Meanwhile, everyone else in school thought the best number should go to the best singer.

Besides, Heather wasn't supposed to even be one of the four leads in the first place. Everyone knew that part was supposed to go to Wren Deslandes. If it weren't for that well-timed call from Heather's father, she would have probably been the head flying monkey. But when Anthony Mayflower says, "Jump," Orion Academy says, "How high does your checkbook go?" And thus, Wren gets to be Glinda #2 while Heather hacks her way through the play in ruby-esque slippers.

"So, what do you think?" Hope asked.

At first I thought she had noticed the intensity of my gaze over at Heather's table. But Hope had already moved past the assumed accident. She was talking to Suze about her dress.

"Chanel?" Suze asked as she looked over the image on the cell phone screen.

Hope nodded.

"I'd say, late forties," Suze added. "Maybe early fifties."

Hope rolled her eyes in my direction. We both knew that Suze was showing off for us.

"Can you do something with it?" Hope asked.

Suze shut the phone and handed it back to Hope, drawing out her response for utmost dramatic effect. "But, of course."

"Great!" Hope said, trying not to look as excited as I knew she felt. Hope has a horrible time finding dresses, but she has an even worse time asking her mom's employees to do her any favors. Having a friend who is was as talented as anyone her mom hires came in handy.

"Let's go shopping for materials right after school," Suze said. I think she was even more excited than Hope.

Did I mention that Suze *loves* fashion?

"We've got rehearsal," Hope reminded her.

"Oh, yeah," Suze said with a fair amount of disappointment, if you ask me. "Then I have piano lessons. We'll have to hold off till the show's finally over."

"And I'll pay you whatever you want," Hope said.

"Just cover the materials," Suze said. "That's fine."

"No," Hope said. "I insist."

"It's fine," Suze said. "I love these projects."

"But I can't take—"

"Show your mom a picture of you in the dress," Suze said. "And be sure to tell her who altered it for you. That's enough."

Hope's face broke into a smile. It was a smile I had seen many times before. Some ingenious plan just popped into her head. "Sure," she said as she dropped her phone back into her bag.

"Miss me?" Sam asked as she slipped in between Eric and Suze.

I could tell Eric and Drew were as surprised as I was to see

Sam slide into her seat. We were so busy watching the painfully cheery nonnegotiations that we hadn't noticed she had come back into the room wearing a new shirt.

One of the perks of having a mom on staff is she tends to keep things on hand for these kinds of emergencies. Sam had probably done a quick dash to her mom's room and pulled something out of her "book" closet, which was much closer to the pavilion than Sam's locker.

"That was fast," I said about Sam's return. I wasn't sure if the need for speed was because she wanted to get back to Eric right away or she wanted to make sure I wasn't left unsupervised with him for too long. Like I would do anything to jeopardize this burgeoning relationship.

If only I had thought of that sooner.

"My lunch is probably getting cold," Suze said as she popped up off the bench. "How about getting together Sunday for materials?"

"I'm free after church," Hope said.

"Perfect," Suze said. "Brunch and then materials shopping."

"Book it," Hope said.

Suze bounced across the aisle to her table and joined the rest of the junior prom committee. Considering the dance didn't take place until the end of the month, prom season seemed to be starting sooner than usual this year. Pretty soon it would be all prom all the time.

Oh, fun.

"What'd I miss?" Sam asked.

"An exciting discussion of fashions of the late forties,"

Drew said. This got him a smack in the head from Hope. "Ouch."

"You should know better by now," I said.

But does the boy learn? Nope. He started reaching in Hope's bag for her phone.

"Come on," he said. "Let me see the picture."

"Not until prom," Hope said, deftly keeping the phone away.

"What, is it, like, bad luck to let your date see the dress before the prom?" he asked.

"No," Hope said, swatting at his hands. "But I like to tease you."

"So we hear," Eric said through a mouthful of taco.

"What!" Hope shrieked. Suddenly, the playfulness stopped as we all wondered exactly how detailed Drew's conversations with Eric were.

"He's making a joke," Drew said as the table did a quick shift and Eric sat straight up. I suspect that Drew just kicked his best friend in the leg.

Drew quickly turned to me. "Don't *you* want to see what the dress looks like?"

"I'm sure she'll show me later," I said, both getting in a dig and getting myself out of the middle of their pending argument.

But Drew wasn't done with using me as a shield yet. "Who are you going to the prom with, anyway?" he asked.

I swear if I ever *do* become a vampire, Drew is the first person I'm putting the bite on.

The uncomfortable silence that followed was interrupted when Suze sprang up from her bench across the way, clutching her throat. Her face was turning a rather deep shade of red. I wish I could say that I had never seen her do that before, but I had. And I knew that it wasn't good.

Appointment with Death

You know how they say that your life flashes before your eyes when you're about to die? For some reason as I stood there watching Suze look like she was about to die, her life flashed in front of *my* eyes. It wasn't her entire life that flashed. Just one very specific moment: the Big Bee Sting Blowup of Freshman Year.

Suze has massive allergy issues. She's been like this for as long as I can remember. She follows a strict diet, avoids being outdoors at certain times, and visits the allergist regularly for shots. Even with all those precautions, a single bee sting had sent her to the hospital for a month at the start of freshman year.

Now, as she dropped to the floor gasping for breath, she looked exactly like she did on that day. Apparently, I wasn't the only one stuck in flashback mode. Everyone else in the lunchroom was standing frozen like me as Suze clutched at the air.

Surprisingly, Jax was the first to react. Springing into action, he dashed across the pavilion and fell to his knees at Suze's side.

Someone yelled, "Her purse!"

Eric ran over to Suze and started rooting through the purse. Meanwhile, Jax ripped open her shirt, popping off buttons and exposing a satin blue bra with beading that matched her outfit so well that I assumed she must have made it that way. It was an odd time for Jax to be copping a feel, but I was still too stunned to actually comment on it aloud.

Eric pulled something out of the bag and handed it to Jax. I couldn't see what it was until Jax lifted his hand above his head, preparing to plunge the thing into her chest. He was holding her emergency injector of epinephrine.

"STOP!" I yelled. With my adrenaline rushing, I stepped up on the bench and bounded over the lunch table in a giant leap, landing at Suze's side.

Dramatic, no?

Truthfully, I was still frozen in place. What actually happened was, I yelled and Drew—having already moved to the other side of the table—grabbed Jax's hand.

Jax looked more confused than usual.

"This is not *Pulp Fiction*," I said as I finally found motion and quickly moved to the other side of the table. Drew took the EpiPen out of Jax's hand and gave it to me. Suze's face was turning blue as I knelt beside her.

Sam was on her other side, holding Suze's hand and keeping her calm.

"You *do* know what you're doing?" Drew asked.

I looked at him. "Everyone get back."

"You heard him!" Hope yelled to the gathering crowd. "Give her some room!"

I looked at the needle in my hand. It was filled with what I hoped was enough epinephrine to stop the vicious allergy attack. I raised her skirt slightly up her thigh, not wanting to add to the humiliation of already having her breasts exposed to the junior and senior classes. Then, I stuck the needle in her thigh.

As the medicine went into her body I saw a look of calm relief wash over Suze's face, replacing the fear that had been there a moment earlier.

"For anaphylactic shock," I said to Jax (and for Drew's benefit as well), "you have to inject the medicine in the thigh or you could cause a cerebral hemorrhage."

Did I mention that the Big Bee Sting Blowup of Freshman Year happened at my birthday party? Having one of your guests nearly die is not something you soon forget.

I could hear Suze's breathing go back to normal. Her face was returning to its typical lightly tanned hue. The crowd—who hadn't bothered to move back at all—looked as relieved as I felt.

"What's going on here?" Mr. Clark, the teacher on duty, asked as he pushed his way through the students, rushing in too late to actually do anything useful. I can only imagine what he thought, seeing a student lying in the middle of the lunchroom with her clothing ripped open and a crowd gathered around her.

Sam quickly pulled Suze's shirt together, and Mr. Clark scattered everyone for real. He sent Jimmy out to get help and within minutes the nurse, headmaster, and assorted administrative personnel were in the lunchroom.

Nobody reacts after-the-fact like the Orion Academy staff.

The students were eventually shooed out to the courtyard to finish our lunch. Normally, we aren't supposed to take food outside—for fear of a stray wrapper littering the grounds—but we were granted a stay on that rule due to the extenuating circumstances of Suze nearly dying.

"That was crazy," Eric said.

"Total Ophelia," Sam agreed.

"Forget Ophelia," I said. "That was a full-on Hamlet."

"Really?" Hope asked. "You think Hamlet was crazier than Ophelia? Most of that craziness was an act to prove his uncle's guilt. And it's not like there weren't extenuating circumstances. But Ophelia was driven to madness about as quickly as Suze's reaction escalated."

Hope did have a point. "How about . . . it was all Lady Macbeth in a full-on sleepwalk?" I asked.

"Exactly!" Hope and Sam agreed.

"You guys are so weird," Drew said.

"Thank you," the three of us said as we all settled on a patch of grass around the William Foster Reflecting Pool and took a seat.

Sam's sandals were off before she hit the ground. "I knew Suze had allergies, but that was intense."

"Not as intense as the first time," Drew said before turning to me. "You remember that? At your birthday party?"

"Why do you think I knew what to do with the EpiPen?" I asked as if it wasn't obvious. Because it *was*. And, by the way, it was a *surprise* birthday party. My mom made the guest list while unaware of certain social realities of the time. Like the fact that having Drew and Eric at my birthday party was the last thing I would have wanted. Even worse, they both showed up like they didn't think anything at all of coming when they totally should have known that they weren't welcome.

"Did anyone hear what caused it?" Hope asked.

Sam had been the nearest to Suze when the nurse arrived, but she hadn't heard anything. No one else had either.

"All we had were the chicken and veggie tacos we have every week," I said. "If she was allergic to anything in those, that would have happened long ago."

The school menu rotates daily, but remains the same week in and week out: Soft Taco Mondays, Burger Tuesdays, Salad Wednesdays, Sandwich Thursdays, and Pizza Fridays. Every day we have veggie and vegan options for the noncarnivores. Other than that, there's really no deviating from the menu. It's weird that Suze would react that way all of the sudden.

As we were about to resume our lunch, we heard sirens approaching. Everyone in the courtyard stopped what they were doing to watch the ambulance drive right up to the pavilion and the EMTs rush out to check on Suze.

Hope looked at what was left of her taco. "Suddenly, I've lost my appetite."

"Me too," Sam and I said in unison, putting down our food as well.

"Hey," Eric said. "Why don't we all grab dinner after practice and rehearsal?"

Not exactly a natural segue when people have just finished saying they aren't hungry.

"What do you say?" Eric persisted, directing his question to Sam. "Your appetite will be back after rehearsal for sure. We can all go."

Sam immediately looked at me.

"We can't," I said. "Toto shopping."

Drew gave me an odd look. "Is that some kind of code?"

"Yes," I said. "It's code for 'We have more important things to do this afternoon.'"

That shut him up.

Okay, I was being childish, but I really didn't care. Thankfully, Sam wasn't saying anything. We didn't actually have *formal* plans for that afternoon. Sam had agreed to go on a props run with me sometime this week. This was the first mention that "sometime" had become "today."

You'd think that, at a school that loans out free laptops at the beginning of the year, we'd have more of a budget for our school show. Yeah. Not so much. To offset the fact that we don't charge for tickets, the budget is kept pretty bare bones. So there's not much money to get stuff with.

It's true that most of us can buy our own props and costumes, but we have far more fun being resourceful about it. It's kind of a tradition. We even give out an award for the best costume or prop found from an unlikely source. So far it looks like this year's award is going to go to Gary McNulty. He's the tenth grader who plays Nikko, the head flying monkey. He's using one of his mom's old fur coats for his monkey costume.

We hoped Tasha's parents won't throw a can of red paint on him in the middle of the show.

Since my mom is all hooked up in the animal world, I offered to pick up some stuffed dogs for our Toto. Mr. Randall wanted four identical dogs so each Dorothy could have her own to work with during the week. Fleischman Brothers Animal Emporium, one of my mom's suppliers, gladly offered to donate the stuffed animals for the show. The only problem is that the Fleischman Brothers work on an appointment-only basis. And they are really hard to pin down for an appointment.

I still hadn't managed to get one.

"Was that today?" Sam asked, like she had forgotten something we both knew I never told her. Thankfully, she didn't call me on it. I suspect that was her way of making up to me for blowing me off about the prom.

"Sorry, Eric," she said. "But I promised. Maybe another time."

"Cool," he said.

I tried not to feel like dirt while Sam covered her look of disappointment.

"I'll be right back," I said as I got up to head to the bathroom.

Once I was out of their sightlines, I made a dash for the school phones. Now, I *really* had to get that appointment.

The Tempest

Mission accomplished!

After trying several numbers my mom gave me for the Fleischman Brothers' workshop and cell phones, I managed to get the senior Fleischman on the phone. He said that he and his brother would be in the studio that afternoon. Sam and I were welcome to come look over their inventory.

Whew.

By the time I hung up the phone, I was more than ready for my next class. It had been a surprisingly eventful lunchtime.

I'm sure you can imagine what the talk was for the rest of the day. More than a few people came up to tell me how cool it was that I, "like, saved Suze's life and all." These were mostly freshmen and sophomores who, I suspect, only wanted to hear what had happened from someone who was there.

Who was I to keep the story from them?

I wasn't entirely comfortable with the sudden fame. Our

school's not large enough for anyone to disappear in a crowd, but I do tend to keep to the fringes. I know it's odd that a Drama Geek doesn't like the spotlight, but that's just me, I guess.

I especially didn't like the spotlight when it found me in Headmaster Collins's office at the end of the day. At first, I thought I was going to get some award for my quick thinking. Maybe a special assembly for heroically saving the life of another.

What? It could happen.

But that idea went out the window as soon as I stepped into the headmaster's office, literally with fedora in hand.

"Please have a seat, Mr. Stark," Headmaster Collins said stiffly as he glanced up at me over his silver-frame glasses.

"Yes, sir," I said, taking one of his guest chairs. I kept my fedora in my lap, not sure if it was rude to wear a hat or not in the headmaster's office. I figured removing it was a "better safe than sorry" move. Besides, it gave me something to twist in my hands as Headmaster Collins spoke to me. For some reason, he always makes me incredibly nervous.

The headmaster drummed his well-manicured fingers on his desk. I swear, Headmaster Collins and his wife are two of the most beautiful people I've ever seen in my life. And I live in a place where beauty is appreciated over anything else. I'm not saying that the two of them have come about this by a natural process. They have both been bronzed, trimmed, sculpted, and injected to within an inch of their lives. So far as I can tell, neither of them has gone under the knife yet, but the amount of money they must spend on teeth bleaching alone could fund a small nation. And don't get me started on their wardrobes.

Maybe that's where the budget for the school show goes.

"You've never been in my office before, have you?" Headmaster Collins asked.

"Not since the admissions interview," I said. That was four years ago, but the place hasn't really changed. Same mod—and thoroughly uncomfortable—furniture. Same trendy artwork on the walls. Same plastic, though intimidating, headmaster.

"You've never been summoned here before for any disciplinary problems."

"No, sir," I said, not entirely sure if it was a question. I just focused on my hat.

"Now, don't get me wrong," he said. This is *never* a good conversation opener. "What you did this afternoon, with Ms. Finberg, is likely to be much appreciated by her family. I suspect they may even wish to show that appreciation in some way. I am sure your friends have probably been patting you on the back through the halls all afternoon."

"I—"

He raised his hand, politely informing me to shut up. It was a good thing too, since I wasn't sure what I was going to say, anyway. I didn't really care if the Finbergs got me anything. And no one had actually patted me on the back since my grandpop died three years ago.

"I know this may appear confusing," the headmaster continued, "but what you did this afternoon, while appreciated by many—including, I'm sure, certain segments of the school faculty—I regretfully have to tell you, was not the best course of action in this case."

I had no idea what he just said.

I mean, really.

Even after I pulled apart his sentence in my head, I still wasn't sure what he was getting at.

"Did I do something wrong?" I asked, looking up from my lap.

"While some might say no," he said, "I am going to have to say, yes."

Let's try this one more time.

"So, I *did* do something wrong?"

"It is against school policy for students to administer any form of medication to one another," he said, clearing up some but certainly not *all* of the reasons I had been summoned.

"But, it was an emergency," I said.

"That is understandable," he replied. "You reacted in the heat of the moment. But have you ever administered epinephrine prior to this afternoon?"

"Well . . . no," I said. "But I saw it done once before." I think the only way I could have sounded any lamer was if I'd added "on TV" to the end of that sentence.

"And did you stop to think for a moment that you could have made things worse?" he asked through a smile that was so bright that it was intimidating on its own.

"I did stop Jax from pumping it straight to her heart," I said weakly, offering up some sort of defense.

"I have already spoken with Mr. Klayton," Headmaster Collins said. "We are discussing *your* actions at the moment."

Considering that we all study in the Klayton Library, I can

imagine *that* conversation had been a little less intimidating. I really need to talk to my parents about buying something around here. Maybe that new light grid. It would certainly make my education considerably less stressful.

"What should I have done?" I asked, going for a more proactive approach.

"Found a teacher and reported the incident so the school nurse could be summoned," he said.

I really didn't want to get Mr. Clark in trouble for not being at his post, but it was either him or me. "There weren't any teachers around at the time."

"Then you should have gone for the nurse yourself," he said. "Or sent one of your friends while you waited with Ms. Finberg."

"But she could have died in the time it took someone to get to the nurse and back," I said.

"She could have died from you administering the drug into her system incorrectly," he said.

"But she didn't."

"But she *could* have."

I guess he took my stunned silence as an apology, because he got up from his seat—brushing the nonexistent wrinkles from his silk suit—and went to the door.

"I knew you would understand," he said as he opened the door.

Still painfully confused, I got up and walked out.

"Please see that you don't do anything else that would have you sent to my office," he said.

"Okay," I replied after the door had shut behind me.

I promise not to save anyone else's life during school hours.

Sam's mom, Anne, was standing in the outer office. At first, I thought it was odd that she was standing right by the door when I came out. It wasn't entirely clear what she was doing there. She certainly wasn't standing around talking to the headmaster's secretary, Mrs. Bell, even though Mrs. Bell was obviously interested in what was going on. You could tell by the way she was leaning forward and staring straight at me as I left the office. Mrs. Bell? Not one for subtlety.

"I had a feeling this would happen," Anne said to me.

I was still pulling myself out of the stunned silence. I think I managed to blink a couple times.

She threw an arm around me, took my fedora out of my hands, and gently placed it back on my head. Usually she refrains from outward signs of affection during school hours, but I suspect she knew I was in some shock. "I'm guessing that Headmaster Collins expressed some concern over what you did this afternoon," she said.

"Kind of."

Anne pulled me out to the empty hall. I guess she didn't like it that Mrs. Bell was still obviously eavesdropping. The woman didn't even bother to hide the fact the she was leaning even farther across her desk. I was afraid she was going to fall out of her seat.

"He thinks he has to say that," Anne said once we were out of earshot. "It's a cover-his-butt type thing. Don't let him make you think you did anything wrong."

"He said I should have gotten the nurse," I said.

"The only thing she's empowered to do is hand out aspirin,"

she said. "Bryan, Suze is going to be perfectly fine. And that's all because of you."

"Really?" I asked.

"Really."

Sure, I had been talking about saving Suze's life all afternoon, but I never really *believed* it until Anne told me I did good.

"Thanks . . . Ms. Lawson," I said. I'm not supposed to call her by her first name at school. "Does anyone know what caused the reaction?"

Anne looked down the hall to make sure no one could overhear. "The headmaster would prefer that this information not get out. So please don't tell anyone," she said. "But there was a mix-up at the restaurant that catered today. A shrimp taco was accidentally sent with the regular order."

"Wow," I said. "Talk about a lawsuit in the making." Shellfish is on the top of the list of things that Suze is allergic to. A fact that Suze's mom had made sure the school knew about back when we started here.

Anne walked me the rest of the way to Hall Hall. I considered asking what she thought of the whole Eric Whitman situation, but decided against it. It was too early to play that card. I wanted to see where this thing was headed before I had to bring in the big guns. She might not even know about it yet. With Anne being a teacher here, Sam already has so much overlap between her school life and her personal life that she doesn't always rush to tell her mom everything.

"I hear I owe you," Anne said. "Sam said I could go home early today."

Sam must have told her about our shopping trip. Anne usually has to wait around until the end of rehearsal to take Sam back to Santa Monica.

"All I ask is that you remember this when I'm in your class next year," I said smoothly, coming out of my headmaster-induced stupor.

"Naturally," Anne said, not meaning it at all. In the world of owing favors, I'm sure I owe her a lot more than she owes me. "Tell my daughter I said hi."

"Will do," I said as I went for the door, leaving Anne out in the hall. I would have asked if she wanted to come in, but I knew better. Sam gets totally flustered when her mom comes to rehearsals.

I checked my watch. Mr. Randall hates it when we're late for rehearsal. I was glad that I had a good excuse, but quickly realized I wouldn't need it. I knew my late entrance would easily be overlooked as soon as I opened the door and heard the chorus of girls' voices in heated discussion. I slipped in totally unnoticed.

Sam and Hope were sitting on the edge of the stage. They were practically the only girls in the cast not encircling Mr. Randall. The chattering girls were all talking over one another so much, I couldn't make out what any of them were saying. Poor Mr. Randall had obviously given up on control. All he could do was stand in silence while they let loose.

"So what are we doing here?" I asked, pointing at the commotion as I joined Sam and Hope onstage.

"Well." Sam leaned in so she could be heard over the noise.

"Since Suze is going to be out for the rest of the week—"

"She's out for the whole week?"

"At *least*."

"You know her mom," Hope added.

"That means we're down a Dorothy," Sam continued. "So Mr. Randall promoted Wren into the role."

"That's great," I said. "Dorothy #4 dances the jitterbug number. Wren is an amazing dancer. Perfect match."

(*Aside:* "The Jitterbug" is a song that was cut from the movie. Check out the two-disc special-edition DVD if you ever want to hear it. It's a really great song.)

I looked over to the seats and saw Wren was already running lines with Jason. I knew she appreciated the part more than Suze had. It was nice that someone in the cast was finally getting what she wanted and deserved. It was also nice that she and her boyfriend were already getting down to work. Considering I was the act two Scarecrow, I would have to offer my services later since Wren would be working with me onstage and not Jason. But Wren and Jason looked like they didn't want to be bothered at the moment.

Those two are an interesting couple. No one would have ever guessed they'd get together. Not because he's Irish and she's Jamaican. This is Malibu, after all. It's because she's a senior, and he's a junior. It goes totally against the rules of high school dating that they'd be a couple. Sure, it's fine for a senior guy to date a junior girl . . . or even a freshman girl. But for some reason, the reverse is not true at all. People would be more scandalized by the age difference if we all

weren't pretty sure they'd break up as soon as Wren gradu-
ates. They totally have the feel of "High School Couple"
about them.

"So *that's* why Heather and Cynthia are so mad," I said,
going back to the commotion.

"They probably thought we'd all get more lines," Sam
added. I suspect she had expected the same thing.

But that didn't explain the rest of the girls. Most of them
were freshmen and sophomores. They couldn't have possibly
expected to be a Dorothy. Leads only go to seniors and juniors since everyone else has two or three more chances for a
starring role before they graduate.

It didn't take long for me to do the necessary cast calcula-
tions to realize what at least part of the commotion was
about.

"So, if Wren is now Dorothy #4, who's playing Glinda #2?"
I asked.

Hope smiled at me and waved with a smug kind of joy.

"You get to be Glinda in *both* acts?" I asked.

She giggled for the second time in a week. At least this
time she was doing it on purpose. Hope was now the only cast
member who would appear in both acts of the play. Not even
the stuffed Totos would get to do that.

"That's why all the *other* girls are complaining," Hope said.
She looked quite pleased with Mr. Randall's decision, and I
couldn't blame her at all.

Toys in the Attic

Mr. Randall eventually got the situation under control and started the rehearsal. Since Hope and Wren were new to act two, we began there and worked our way backward.

The difference in dynamic was totally noticeable with Wren in the role of Dorothy. Suze is an amazing actress. She's got this innate talent that I would die for. The thing that really kills me is, she doesn't care. She has no interest in being on the stage at all, so she pretty much walks her way through the scenes. I'm not saying she purposely doesn't try, but she does kind of phone it in.

Wren, on the other hand, worked for every moment. You could actually see her connect with the nuances of her character. She really gave you something to work off. The first time Wren said to me (as the Scarecrow) that she'd miss me most of all, I totally believed it.

And you should see her move. We like to joke that she's

been dancing since before she could walk, but I honestly wouldn't be surprised if that was true. We were moving through the second part of the second act rather well with Wren in the role. I don't think the same could be said for everyone else.

There were actually several rehearsals going on at the same time, one per Dorothy. While we worked on the end of act two with Mr. Randall, Sam and Cindy worked on their scenes with whoever was available. Meanwhile, Ms. Monroe, the music teacher-assistant director, tried to coax vocal talent out of Heather.

From what I could hear, Ms. Monroe was failing.

Miserably.

Eventually Mr. Randall called an end to the main rehearsal because he needed the stage to work on the jitterbug dance number with Wren. Since he now had a trained dancer in the part, he wanted to try out some new choreography. Luckily, he didn't want the rest of us in the scene to stick around. Sam and I had to get to the Fleischmans.

After the tragic lunch earlier, our spirits were so lifted by the rehearsal that Sam led everyone in a rousing rendition of "We're Off to See the Wizard" as we left the theater. There is nothing like the sound of two dozen Drama Geeks' voices raised in song, echoing through the empty halls in the late afternoon. I guess Headmaster Collins felt differently, because he hurried out of his office to quiet us down right when we got to the "because, because, because, because, becaaaauuuse" part.

The group quickly dispersed and I was alone with my two best friends, who were still stuck on what I had told them earlier about my last run-in with the headmaster.

"I can't believe he had the nerve to act like you did something wrong," Hope said as we left school together.

"Yeah, but I'm over it," I said nobly (in my opinion). "I'm more concerned about Suze."

Hope shook her head sadly. "Nearly killed by a rogue shrimp taco."

"Talk about a lawsuit in the making," Sam echoed my earlier comment.

See why we're such good friends?

Let me interject for a moment to clarify: I knew when Anne told me not to tell anyone about the shrimp taco earlier, she meant anyone *other than* Sam and Hope.

"You sure you don't want to come with us?" I asked Hope as we hit the parking lot. "The Fleischman Brothers are a kick."

"You know how I feel about riding on the freeway in your death trap," Hope said.

"Hey! Not so loud. She'll hear you." I played being insulted, but I had expected that response.

"It's not like she doesn't know how I feel about her," Hope said as we worked our way through the student parking lot. Filled with Hummers and hybrids, it was like an ecological battleground of trendiness. With one notable exception:

Electra.

"Hi, sexy," I said as I reached my baby, safely parked along the far edge of the lot, away from the masses.

Electra is a red and white 1957 Ford Fairlane Skyliner with a silver streak running down the sides. She's even got a convertible hard top, although the top hasn't been able to convert since before I was born. My grandpop left Electra to me when he died. True, she's not the most *ecologically* sound car in the world, but she's got style. Even Hope appreciates that and loves to be seen tooling around Malibu in her.

Hope's problem with Electra is when I take her out on the freeway. Since Electra is so . . . mature of age . . . she was born at a time before seat belts were standard. That coupled with the fact that Electra takes some time deciding whether she wants to brake or not makes Hope a little nervous.

Can't imagine why.

"I'm going to hitch a ride with Drew," Hope said as she veered off toward the soccer field. Since we got out of rehearsal early, they still had a half hour of practice to go.

"Tell him we said hi," Sam said.

I waited.

"And Eric, too," Sam added.

I did a very good job at not gagging as we boarded Electra and headed on our way.

The Fleischman Brothers' studio was in Burbank, which is a straight shot down the 101 to the 134. Considering that rush hour in the L.A. area runs from three o'clock to sometime after seven, we were hitting the freeway at the height of the traffic. It took us close to an hour and a half to get there. This is why I don't understand Hope not wanting to come with us. How bad of an accident could we get into going four miles an hour?

We used the car time to run the second act since I didn't exactly have it committed to memory yet. Memorization isn't one of my strong suits. It's even more difficult when your best friend already knows the entire play, including the parts she's not in. By the time we pulled into the small parking lot behind Fleischman Brothers Animal Emporium, I had a much better handle on my part.

"This is it?" Sam asked skeptically. We were outside a small warehouse in an industrial section by the train tracks and the 5 freeway.

"You know what they say about a book and its cover," I said, getting out of the car.

There was a sign beside the door that asked us to ring the bell for service. I pressed the button, looked at Sam, and we both went, "Who rang that bell?" like the doorman from the Emerald City. Then we broke down in the kind of hysterical laughter that probably would have annoyed everyone we know, except Hope.

"Bryan! So good to see you!" the elder Fleischman Brother said as he opened the door. "How's your mother?"

"She's fine, Mr. Mariano," I said. As we entered, Sam gave me a weird look.

"Tell her we're working on the fall line of stuffed dogs and should have a preview for her soon," he said.

"Will do."

"And who is this lovely young lady?" he asked, eyeing Sam.

"This is my friend Sam," I replied.

"Hello, Mr. . . . Mariano?" Sam asked.

"Please, call me Tony," he replied, taking her hand. While he was still holding her hand, Tony leaned over to me and said in a rather loud whisper that Sam could easily hear, "Is she a *special* friend?"

"Just a friend," I said with a smile. We get that a lot.

"Well, now, any friend of Bryan's . . ." Tony turned and pushed open the double doors to the showroom.

"Wow!" was all Sam could say.

"See what I meant about a book and its cover," I whispered.

"It's . . ."

"Yes," I said. "It is."

I knew exactly how she felt. I was six the first time I was in the Fleischman Brothers' showroom and I still remember the overwhelming feel of it all. True, a stuffed animal palace would impress most six-year-olds, but I've been back to the Fleischmans' place numerous times since then and I have still never seen anything else like it in my life.

Imagine a bright-white car showroom with a sparkling marble floor. All along the floor, where the cars would be, stand nearly life-size lions, tigers, bears, and other stuffed animals too big to fit on any shelf or hug while asleep. The white walls are filled with lit cubbyholes showing off smaller stuffed cats, birds, and more styles of teddy bears than you could ever imagine. Now, triple the size of the showroom you've imagined and you'll start to have an idea of what the reality is like.

"It's amazing," Sam finally managed to whisper loudly enough for us to hear.

Tony was beaming proudly.

The Fleischman Brothers are known throughout the world for the stuffed animal creations they've been designing for decades. They really are works of art. All the prototypes are made by hand, then sent to their factory in Minnesota for mass production before being shipped all over the world. The small Burbank warehouse is where it all starts.

"Jacob, don't be rude!" Tony yelled—quite loudly—into the back workroom. "We have guests!"

"In a minute!" Jacob yelled back.

Don't think the yelling was simply because they were calling to each other across a large room. Or the fact that they are older men and hard of hearing. The Fleischman Brothers can hear just fine, they just like to yell at each other. I guess that comes from being in business together since World War II.

"I swear, Jacob is going to be the death of me with his horrible manners," Tony said—loudly—to me. Then he yelled back, "At least say hi to Bryan and his young lady friend."

"Hi, Bryan and his young lady friend," Jacob echoed back.

"Hi, Mr. Miller!" I called back, trying not to laugh.

"Hi!" Sam yelled. She looked at me with the same confused face she had earlier. "Um . . . who's Mr. Fleischman?"

Tony and I shared a laugh. I would have explained it to Sam earlier, but the Fleischman Brothers do so love telling their story.

"We're both Mr. Fleischmans," Tony said. "Except we're not."

"Okaaay," Sam said, clearly clueless.

"Mr. Fleischman is our father-in-law," he explained.

"*Was* our father-in-law," Jacob corrected as he came out of the workroom. "And he was no father-in-law of mine."

"He was too," Tony said before turning to Sam with a conspiratorially loud whisper. "Jacob's mad because Papa Fleischman liked me best."

"That old man didn't like nobody," Jacob said. "'Specially not the two men who dared to marry his little angels."

"That's kind of true," Tony admitted.

I had met both their wives a few years back. They are just as loud as their husbands. I can only imagine what their father was like.

Much as the faux Fleischman Brothers were enjoying their routine, it *had* been a long drive to the showroom and I was getting hungry. I tried to hurry things along. "Mr. Fleischman Senior started Fleischman's Animal Emporium back in the twenties."

"He was one of the first to mass-produce stuffed animals on an assembly line," Tony said with pride.

"And the first to price-gouge on kiddie toys," Jacob added, with considerably less pride.

"He took us on as kids," Tony explained. "That's how we met our wives. When he passed, he left us the business."

"And gave us the business too, if you know what I mean," Jacob said. "Man couldn't manage a budget to save his life. We brought this company out of near bankruptcy, stabilized the pricing, and made it the success it is today."

"Mom only buys her dog models from the Fleischman Brothers," I said. Tony and Jacob both beamed. "Which is why

I knew they'd be the perfect guys to go to for help with our play."

As we say in L.A.: Flattery can get you free stuff.

"Right this way," Tony said as he led us across the show-room. "Not everybody gets to go up to the stockroom, you know. It's only 'cause we've known you 'bout near all your life now, Bryan."

"I'm honored, Tony," I said, and meant every word. So honored, in fact, that it took me a moment to realize that we were heading to the workroom. I think my feet were the first to notice, because they stopped in their tracks before I reached the doorway. I could feel the blood run out of my face. "We have to go in *there?*" My voice trembled with fear.

"That's the only way to get to the storeroom," Tony said calmly as he passed through the Threshold to Hell.

I grabbed Sam before she could follow. "Whatever you do, *don't* look at the room. Look at your feet. Look at the ceiling. Keep your hand at the level of your eyes. Whatever it takes. Just *don't look.*"

Sam laughed. *She laughed!* "Bryan, knock it off."

"I'm serious. Trust me."

"Sure," she said. "Whatever."

I didn't think she was going to listen.

Still laughing, Sam crossed into the workroom. *Oh, the horror.* I took a deep breath and followed, keeping my eyes squarely focused on my shoes the entire time.

I had only been in the Fleischman Brothers' workroom once before. When I was eight. I still have the terrifying images burned into my brain. There is nothing in the world that can prepare a child for the absolute horror of dozens of very real-looking stuffed animals with their innards spilling out onto the tables and floors. The severed limbs and tails and ears scattered about the room are enough to make you lose your lunch. It's worse than any horror movie I've ever seen. Following my last visit, I had nightmares for months. I haven't been able to enter a Build-A-Bear Workshop since.

But that's not the worst of it.

The truly horrific part is the eyes.

Step by step, I made my way through the workroom, looking at nothing but the floor. I could feel the empty beaded eyes of the rows and rows of decapitated animal heads watching me from the shelves.

This would be one of the downsides of having an overactive imagination.

Eventually, we made it through the room and into the small stairwell beyond. Even though the Fleischmans had been the only ones talking while we were in the workroom, I knew that Sam hadn't listened to me about not looking. I prepared myself to be there for my friend when I finally looked up from my shoes to see her face.

Surprisingly, the mask of fright I had expected was not there. I thought it was possible that she had been simply too stunned to react.

"Are you okay?" I gently asked.

"They were stuffed animals," she said with no quiver in her voice whatsoever. "Seriously. Not that scary."

"But . . ."

She put a hand on my shoulder, "Come on, Tarzan."

"This way," Tony said brightly as he took us upstairs.

I shook off my confusion as Tony and Sam led the way, leaving Jacob and me to bring up the rear. In much the same way his brother-in-law spoke in a stage whisper, Jacob asked, "So, is this young lady a *special* friend?"

I could see Sam's back rising and falling in front of me as she held back the laughter.

I echoed what I had told Tony, but stopped short once we reached the stockroom. I was literally struck speechless. The showroom was one thing, but this stockroom was unimaginable.

It ran the length of the entire building, and the ceiling was twice as high as the first floor. Hundreds upon hundreds of shelves rose up from the floor all the way to the roof. They were piled with stuffed animals that must have dated back to Mr. Fleischman's early days. There was row after row after row of everything from tiny toys to larger-than-life-size replicas, including two horses rearing back in front of the doorway as if they were guarding the sanctum.

"Dogs are two rows down." Tony waved to the right. "The stockroom is divided by animal and then by breed. You'll find terriers about three quarters of the way back. Take whatever you want."

"Thank you so much, guys," I said.

Sam and I started toward the dog row, but Jacob grabbed me to hold back for a second.

"Just so you know, the ladies love it with all the stuffed cuties," he said. "The wife and I have had many a romantic interlude up here."

Okay . . . *eww!*

"This is the most adorable thing I've ever seen," Sam said as she grabbed onto a stuffed collie and hugged it like it was a real dog.

Apparently, Jacob knew of what he spoke.

And . . . *ewww* . . . again.

"What do you think of Toto being a collie?" Sam asked. "You know, considering we have four different Dorothys and all. Who would complain?"

"I think it's quite possible that if we come back with anything other than a dog that looks like Toto as Mr. Randall imagines him, we might make our teacher cry."

Sam put the collie back on the shelf. "Good point."

We continued down the row past the dachshunds and dalmatians, the German shepherds and poodles, until we finally reached the terriers.

There were terriers of all sizes and colors. The organizational system was impressive. We found a great selection of black terriers easily at a shelf that was eye level. It was a good thing too. I didn't want to have to climb one of the ladders to get to the top shelf all the way up by the peaked roof of the warehouse.

"This is too perfect," Sam said as she grabbed at the dogs.

"Do I know where to go, or what?"

"You are the doggie master," Sam said.

I wasn't quite sure how to take that.

We grabbed four terriers and made our way back down to the showroom. This time, I forced myself to keep my eyes open and focused ahead of me as we walked through. I figured if Sam could do it, I could too. Honestly, I was still a little freaked by the disembodied heads, but it was not really as horrifying as I remembered. They were only cloth, beads, and stuffing, after all.

Once we got back to the showroom, we saw that Tony was holding a plush white unicorn with a silver horn. He had a huge grin on his face. I mean Tony, not the unicorn.

"For the little lady," Tony said. "To match your necklace."

"Oh no, I couldn't."

"'Course you can," Jacob said. "A little something special for Bryan's special friend."

This is what I don't get about some people. I've told them twice that Sam isn't my "special" friend. But here they are trying to put us together. With cute little stuffed gifts, even. Now, imagine for a moment that I was, in fact, straight. And imagine I had some secret crush on Sam. And further imagine that she had no interest in me at all.

I know that last one is a lot to imagine, but stay with me here.

Don't you think it would be kind of hurtful to keep pushing her on me?

Sam took the toy. "Thank you."

"Now, you two kids get going," Tony said. "The night is young."

I didn't bother to remind them that the night got a little older when you factored in the drive all the way back to Malibu and Santa Monica. Sam and I left, but we hit the food court at the Burbank Town Center Mall before getting back on the freeway. I'm not usually big on fast food, but any meal that doesn't include Eric Whitman is a five-star dining event as far as I'm concerned.

The Front Page

"**Did you ever feel like you're really close to figuring**
something out but there's, like, this wall that's in your way? You
know there's an answer on the other side, but you can't get to it
at all," Hope asked as the two of us went out to the courtyard.

"Every day," I said as I took a seat on the grass beside her.
So far, lunch hadn't been nearly as eventful as the day before.
Not one person had come close to dying.

Eric and Drew had joined us once again. Drew's been dating Hope on and off for—well, it seems like *ever*—and this was
the first time he'd eaten with us two days in a row. And he
probably wouldn't have if Eric hadn't suggested it.

I was concerned that Drew was the wall Hope was talking
about. The two of them were cute together, but I just didn't
see this as the greatest love of all time or anything like that.
There just didn't seem to be a romantic connection, a spark.
But I wasn't ready for *that* conversation.

Thankfully the guys didn't follow us out to the courtyard. Sam had to talk to her mom about something, so Eric and Drew went off to work on some project, leaving me and Hope to talk about whatever was bothering her.

"I hate this play," Hope finally said as she pulled out her script.

I tried not to look relieved that she wasn't planning to have a more serious conversation.

"Having trouble finding your character?"

"Glinda's such a smug little priss, don't you think?"

"The script just says she's a good witch," I said. "Doesn't mean she's nice."

"All along, she has the way for Dorothy to get home," Hope ranted. "Who is *she* to withhold that information? The poor girl is worried about her family, but all Glinda cares about is teaching Dorothy a lesson."

"Well, it *is* a dream," I explained. "Glinda could represent Dorothy's conscience. Dorothy knew she was being whiny before the twister and she has to learn to appreciate what she's got."

"And these song lyrics," Hope went on. "There's no such thing as a ding-a-berry! I looked it up!"

Somehow, I don't think Hope was really that upset about the play. Maybe she *had* noticed Drew's sudden interest in eating with us was suspiciously tied to Eric's interest in Sam. Drew isn't always the most sensitive when it comes to other people's feelings. It's not like he's intentionally cruel, just oblivious. Trust me. I know what I'm talking about here.

Hope was waiting for me to say something. "Look . . . I . . ."

Yeah. I had nowhere to go with that. Hope and I don't really do *serious*.

"Sorry," Sam said as she arrived, saving us from a real conversation. "Mom stuff."

"You were gone, like, three seconds," I said, dramatically checking my watch. "I think we can manage without you for that long."

"Shut it," she said with a smile.

"Although some people obviously can't," I added.

Yep. The Abercrombie Zombies, Eric and Drew, were heading our way in their almost matching ensembles of khaki shorts and faded T's. The only difference between the outfits was that Eric's shirt was maroon, while Drew's was this really amazing shade of blue that totally made his eyes pop. I was having a hard time not staring right into them.

Not that I noticed.

"Don't you guys *ever* separate?" I asked as they plopped down a few feet away from us and opened up Eric's laptop.

"Don't you?" Drew asked, looking over at Sam, Hope, and me.

"Point taken," I ceded.

"Didn't you want to go over lines?" Sam asked Hope in an obvious attempt to break the mounting dramatic tension.

Hope held up her script. "Please."

We quickly ran through the end of the play a couple times so Hope could try some different things with line reads and such. I shared Hope's script, but Sam waved us off. That whole being off book thing was starting to get annoying.

(*Aside*: As the name indicates, "off book" means when an actor no longer needs to read from a script.)

We were doing fairly well at first, but Hope's line reads got more and more intense the further along we read. It was clear that Hope hadn't quite found her character yet. She had a real problem committing to the sugary sweet character made famous in the movie. When she finally yelled, "Yes! And Toto, too, you spoiled, selfish, whiny little baby!" we figured it was time to take a break.

"Isn't that the end of the play?" Eric asked as soon as we stopped.

"Yes," Sam replied.

"But, aren't you just in the first act?"

"Yes."

"You memorized the whole play?"

Sam blushed.

"Wow."

What*ever*.

"I like to work with the whole script," Sam explained. "Get down my character's motivation."

"It's *The Wizard of Oz*," I reminded her. "Dorothy's motivation is to get home."

"You know what I mean," she said, without even looking back at me.

Sam takes acting very seriously. Just because it was a high school show with four girls sharing the same part didn't mean she wasn't going to work it like it was Broadway. I've always thought that was impressive, with maybe a little side of obsessive.

"I apologize, dear thespian," I said with my best British accent. "And I tip my fedora to you." And I did just that.

"Is there some reason you can't just call it a hat?" Drew asked.

"Peasant." I shot him my most withering glare, the one I save for people who are seriously beneath contempt.

"What's wrong with your face?" he asked. "Don't tell me you're having an allergic reaction, too."

I could feel my teeth clenching. Drew is well aware that it was my grandpop's fedora, and how much it means to me. We do not make fun of the fedora.

"Anybody hear how Suze's doing?" Sam quickly asked before I exploded.

Eric and Drew took the question as an invitation to slide over and merge our two groups. They were still working on the computer, but their focus wasn't really on their work. It was on Sam and Hope.

Once again I got the feeling that I had disappeared.

While they talked about Suze's health and well-being, I checked out what was going on in the courtyard. There was a sudden flurry of activity as people ran from group to group talking animatedly about something. I noticed more than a few laptops seemed to be the focal point.

"Suze's home from the hospital," Hope said. "I'm bringing my dress over to her this afternoon so she can get a feel for what she wants to do with it."

"That's okay?" Sam asked. "After yesterday?"

"She's already bored out of her mind," Hope said. "She's dying for something to do. Sorry. Bad choice of words."

"But she's not allowed to come back to school?" Sam asked.

Hope simply shrugged. That was typical of Suze's mom. The woman is a smidge overprotective.

I wasn't really paying attention to the conversation. All that movement and mumbling had suddenly stopped. The place had gotten very, very quiet.

I scanned the courtyard more closely. Now, everyone was huddled in groups around their laptops. I doubted that they were looking at breaking world news.

"Oh. My. God," Drew said.

Both he and Eric were staring at the screen of the iBook with pretty much the same look that everyone else around us had. I guess Sam and Hope also caught up with what was going on, because they looked at me like we were the only ones out of the loop.

Which, I guess, we were.

The three of us quickly slid over so we could see the screen of Eric's laptop. The guys shifted slightly out of the way so we could get a peek. Needless to say, we weren't quite expecting what we saw.

Let me back up for a second.

Every student is loaned a laptop at the beginning of the school year. Our school is a WiFi hotspot, and all the computers are programmed to open up on the school's home page when we go online. Naturally there are "safeguards" in place to catch us if we ever use the school computers to surf for porn.

Apparently, there's nothing in place to stop the porn from coming to us.

Because, looking at the screen, we were all shocked to see a slideshow with naked pictures of Cindy Lakeside on the school's home page.

I'm sorry . . . *Cynthia.*

"Wow," I said in awe.

"Bryan!" Hope and Sam yelled at me, then slammed the laptop closed.

"I can't believe you," Sam said.

Hope smacked me on the shoulder.

"They were staring too," I said, in my own defense. What? Like I wasn't supposed to have a reaction when one of the most beautiful girls in the entire school was splashed naked on a computer screen in front of me?

Okay . . . actually, the "wow" was more in reference to the shots themselves than Cindy's naked body. What little I saw was pretty amazing. The balance of light and shadow was subtle enough to kick Cindy's natural beauty up to stunning. The pictures were clearly taken by a true artist.

My attempt to get Eric and Drew in trouble along with me was all for naught, because, at that very moment, Cindy came strolling out to the courtyard. From the way she was laughing and carrying on with Wren, she had no clue that she was the new online pinup girl.

It only took her a moment to realize that every head in the

courtyard was staring at her. Then looking at their computer screens. Then staring at her again.

And here's why Cindy impresses the hell out of me.

She took it all in.

She came to a conclusion.

She pushed her way into the nearest group to look at what they were ogling.

A brief flicker of shock crossed her face before she went totally emotionless.

Then she stood up tall and strolled out of the courtyard without looking back.

That's when the silence of the past two minutes erupted.

How to Succeed in Business Without Really Trying

"I can't *believe* Mr. Randall thinks the play is cursed," I said as we left the theater.

"I can't *believe* he canceled rehearsal," Hope said as we fell in step on the way to her locker. The play opens—"

"And closes—"

"On Saturday."

"But he needs to work with the Dorothys," I reiterated his reasoning. "I'm sorry. But *I* still haven't gotten the new choreography for the jitterbug."

"And *I* still don't know how he wants me to make my entrance in act two!" Hope said as we reached her locker. "This is ridiculous!" She punctuated her statement by slamming her fist into her locker.

We spent a moment glaring at each other.

"Feel better?" I asked.

"Yeah," she said. "You?"

"Much."

No one had seen Cindy since lunch. Various reports had her storming off campus in tears or throwing a fit in front of Headmaster Collins. Personally, I couldn't see Cindy doing either of those things. The rumor I *did* believe was that she was so mortified by the nude pictures that she wasn't planning on showing herself around here for the rest of the week. At least, that's what Mr. Randall had been told.

The result: a new shift in the Dorothy roles.

"I can't believe Mr. Randall gave Sam all of act one," Hope said.

I shrugged. It made perfect sense to me.

Mr. Randall was busy turning the jitterbug number into this huge dance exhibition for Wren. It was almost like he had given up on the entire play and was focusing on nothing but that dance. He certainly wasn't going to expand Heather's role any. He'd want to keep her total suckage to a minimum to lessen the damage to the play. That left the first act to Sam.

Of course, the other girls in the cast weren't exactly happy with that plan. Especially when Mr. Randall canceled the afternoon's rehearsal to work with the Dorothys. Actually, nobody in the cast liked that part. We were nowhere near ready for Saturday's show, but instead of doing whatever we could to fix that problem, we were all sent home.

Just use the time to go over your lines, he had said.

Hope tried to open her locker, but it was jammed shut.

"Guess it doesn't like to be hit," I said.

She glared at me through the narrowed slits in her eyelids as she reworked the combination.

"I thought the rest of the girls were going to freak when Randall said he wasn't promoting anyone else to a Dorothy," I said.

Hope pulled at her locker again. It opened slightly, but not all the way. "We can't keep changing everyone's roles," she said. "At some point we've got to lock this thing down so we can be ready for tech."

She was right. Our all-day technical rehearsal was two days away and we still hadn't had a single run-through of the entire play from start to finish.

Hope finally yanked her locker open all the way. "Maybe the play *is* cursed."

"You don't really—"

"Stranger things have happened."

"Sure," I said. "Maybe the lamp falling, and Suze accidentally eating a shrimp taco when she's deathly allergic . . . okay . . . *those* could be accidents. But someone went in and put those naked pictures of Cynthia on the school website. That wasn't any curse. That was just cruel."

"True," Hope said.

"Someone did that on purpose," I added, not liking where this line of thought was taking me.

Apparently, it was taking Hope to the same place. "You don't think someone is sabotaging the play."

"*Or* sabotaging the Dorothys," I said, coming to that conclusion on the spot.

"That's ridiculous."

"And having four girls cast in one role *isn't* ridiculous," I said.

"That lamp could have killed someone," Hope said. "I doubt anyone would go that far."

Maybe I *was* being a bit overly dramatic, but it was weird that these things kept happening to the Dorothys.

"What was up with those photos, anyway?" I asked.

I hadn't expected an answer, but Hope had a look on her face that told me she had clearly done some research. I'm not embarrassed to admit that a shiver of excitement ran up my spine over the potential gossip. "What's the tale, nightingale?"

"Well," she said, "according to Wren, Cindy had them done on her eighteenth birthday. I guess she was keeping it a secret and hoping that someday in the future when she got famous, the photos would accidentally come out and cause all sorts of scandal."

"Thus making her even more famous," I added.

"Exactly," she said. "Some guy named Leonard Brock took them."

"That's why they looked so good," I said. Brock is *the* hot new guy on the fashion photography scene. My mom nearly went into hysterics when he agreed to shoot her doggie designs for a spread for *ELLE* on supermodels and their dogs.

It figures that Cindy would only go to the best for a scandal.

"You going to see Suze now?" I asked. "I'm sure she's dying to hear about what happened today."

"Right after I pick up her homework," Hope said. "Anne collected it all for me."

"Mind if I tag along?" I asked.

"I was hoping you'd ask. I could use a lift." Hope had no problem riding in Electra as long as we kept to the back roads of Malibu.

"Glad I can help." I felt for Hope. Especially since I had been in her situation not so long ago. California has this stupid law that for the first six months after getting a driver's license, underage drivers can't drive with their friends in the car unless there's an adult present. They can drive alone fine, but what fun is that?

My six-month probation ended about six weeks ago. Since Hope had been in Paris for the summer over her sixteenth birthday she didn't have a chance to go for her driving test until winter break. She's still got more than a month to go before she can drive with her friends in the car. Since she can only drive by herself, the steps get first dibs on the spare family car. This leaves Hope stuck with bumming rides from people.

Hope slammed her locker shut. She had to do it twice before the lock caught.

"I have to swing by my locker." Which was in the opposite direction. "I'll meet you at Anne's office."

I watched Hope head down the hall for a moment before I turned to go to my locker. She was right about the lamp falling. It was too dangerous for someone to have done it on purpose. Not to mention that Suze's reaction to the shrimp taco could have killed her too. No matter how intense the children of the rich and famous get around here at times, no one would actually commit murder over the school show.

Then again, it's not like people around here actually think anything through. I can imagine any number of my beloved classmates who would drop a lighting instrument on someone entirely unaware that it could do serious damage.

Heather, for instance.

That last thought was running through my head as I went for my locker. It didn't stay too long because as soon as I turned the corner, I saw Cindy at her locker. I was surprised that she was still around.

She probably didn't want anyone bothering her, but I was dying to know about those pictures. "Hey, Cindy."

She tensed up visibly. "Cynthia. Please."

"Sorry," I said. "I've been calling you Cindy since grade school. It's kind of hard to switch it like that."

"I know," she said. "But I'm trying to book modeling gigs. I don't want people thinking I'm a little girl anymore."

I'm guessing the naked photos will help with that.

"How are you?" I asked.

"Saw the pictures, huh?" She let out a forcibly lighthearted laugh. "Who am I kidding? The whole school saw them."

"It's not the end of the world, you know," I said. "Nothing to quit the show over."

"Right. Like I'm going to walk onstage in front of everyone after they saw me like that."

"It's not as bad as you think," I said. "The pictures were actually quite beautiful. The way the light reflected off your skin. It was like you were glowing. And you looked so comfortable . . . so natural. It's honestly some of your best work . . . I mean, you know . . . not that I . . ."

"Thanks," she said, saving me from my embarrassed stumbling. "But I'd rather spend the next few days hiding out at home. Let it all blow over."

Honestly, I couldn't blame her. If naked pictures of me— okay, you know what . . . I'm not even going to let my mind go there.

"How did they get on the site, anyway?" I asked. I figured if someone was sabotaging the Dorothys, Cindy—Cynthia— might have a clue or something.

"Damned if I know," she said. "I was keeping the CD with the shots in my locker so my parents wouldn't find them at home."

"Who knows your combination?"

"Doesn't matter." Cynthia shut her locker, turned the lock, and reopened it without bothering to put in the combination. "It's been like that since I got it."

Not surprising. Half the lockers around school are just as bad.

"Of course, now my folks know all about the photos," she said.

"What did they say?"

"They were cool," she said. "Actually, my dad thought one or two of them might be good to include in my portfolio."

Am I the only one disturbed by that statement?

I chose to lock that concern away in the part of my brain I try not to visit often. Instead, I focused on the positive. "See?

Your folks are fine with it. Everyone around here probably is too. It's hardly any worse than that bathing suit you wore to the end-of-the-year picnic last year."

"I *did* look good in that," Cindy said. "It was La Perla." She had this fond look of recollection on her face that was so perfect, I was pretty sure she had practiced it in a mirror.

"You can't go into hiding," I said. "You're letting the person who put up those pictures win by forcing you out of the show. You are so much better than that."

Cindy looked at me for a moment. Then she gave me a smile that probably would have filled most guys' dreams.

"You are *so* not like normal guys," she said.

I can't tell you how often I get that particular *compliment.* "Thanks."

"No, I mean it," she said, adding insult to the . . . well . . . insult. "I ran into Jax earlier and he was all 'Hey, nice rack.'"

I tried to ignore the fact that she considered Jax a *normal* guy.

"Okay, look"—she checked the hall to make sure we were alone—"if I tell you something, do you promise not to tell anyone?"

I couldn't wait to hear where this was going. I knew Sam and Hope would love whatever it was when I told them. "Sure," I lied.

"I'm not really going into hiding," she said.

"Then—"

"Somehow, a booking agent saw the photos on the web."

Somehow? A booking agent? Saw photos on our school website?

"Victoria's Secret is flying me out to New York tomorrow for their next catalog," she said. She was bouncing up and down on the balls of her feet in excitement. "Did you ever think you'd see me in *Vicky's Secret!*"

I could honestly say that that thought had never crossed my mind. Unlike, I'm sure, many of the *normal* boys at our school.

"I just had to come back for the original CD," she said as she took the disc with what I assume had dozens of naked photos of her on it out of her locker. Oh, the number of guys who would kill to have a few minutes with that disc. "The photographer wanted to match the look."

"But why the act?" I asked. "Why don't you just tell everyone the photos don't bother you in the least?"

"I've already used up more than my share of excused absences for modeling gigs," she said. "If I miss any more school, I'm going to have to make up work over the summer."

Suddenly, the dawn came. "And this way you can use the fact that Headmaster Collins probably feels horrible over pictures showing up on the school website to cut you some slack on the unexcused absences."

"Exactly," she said with a happy little shrug. "Besides, Sam totally deserves to get act one to herself. It's not like she has all that much going for her besides her talent."

It was amazing how Cindy could be both condescendingly thoughtful and totally self-serving at the same time. I immediately stopped worrying about her. Cindy would be perfectly fine. *Cynthia* would see to that.

"Congratulations," I said.

"Thanks," she replied. "And thanks for being so . . . not typical."

I shrugged my shoulders. What else could I do?

"Later, Bryan," she said as she moved down the hall with a spring in her step. Obviously, she had been rehearsing her runway walk.

"Later, Cind-ithia."

Design for Living

"Bryan Stark, you get in here this minute!" Mrs. Finberg said as she pulled me in the front door and gave me a hug that cut off the circulation to the lower part of my body.

"Good to see you, too," I said. Though it came out more like, "Moom mo mee moo moo," considering how my face was smashed into her shoulder at the time.

"Hi, Mrs. Finberg," Hope said, temporarily forgotten in the doorway.

"Hello, Hope." Mrs. Finberg finally released me. "I'm sorry you both came out here, but Suze isn't ready for guests yet."

"I wanted to return this dress she loaned me," Hope said as she held up the outfit that she had bought over the weekend. We had rehearsed this bit in the car, so I waited for my cue.

"Please don't tell me that's another one of her creations," Mrs. Finberg said. I could hear the disdain in her voice. "I swear, that girl has got to learn to make better use—"

"No," Hope jumped in. "It's something she picked up at a consignment shop. It was for a scene we were doing in drama class. She thought it would look better on me."

"Oh! A scene? What play?" Mrs. Finberg asked, ignoring the fact that Hope's body would have a difficult time fitting into any dress her daughter would get for herself. Any talk about Suze doing any kind of acting set her mom's heart aflutter.

Mrs. Finberg could give Mama Rose a run for the money in the stage mom department.

"*The Miracle Worker*," Hope said.

Mrs. Finberg's eyes lit up with excitement. "Come in, come in!" She ushered us into the huge living room and took a seat on the couch. Hope and I remained standing. We didn't want her to think we were staying. At least, not in the living room.

"Suze never tells me about her scene work," Mrs. Finberg said, literally sitting on the edge of her seat. "Which part did she play? No. Don't tell me. She had to be Helen Keller. Such a challenging role. Not that I don't think you could play it, dear. But Suze is much more the ingenue type, don't you think?"

I took that as my cue. Hope would probably have killed Mrs. Finberg if she went any further. "Since we're here," I said, "are you sure Suze can't see anyone? Even for a few minutes?"

"Doctor's orders," Mrs. Finberg replied.

I've known this family long enough to know the "doctor" here was actually Mrs. Finberg. She worries incessantly about her children. Although, considering a tiny insect is a threat to Suze's very life, I guess I can't blame her for being over-protective.

"I understand," I said with a pout. "I was just concerned. You know, I haven't seen her since I gave her that injection. I just wanted to make sure she was okay."

"She's doing wonderfully," Mrs. Finberg said happily, to ease my mind.

"It's just . . . it was so scary," I said, pouring it on even thicker. "Seeing her like that. Are you sure we can't pop in for a minute?"

"Well . . ."

"We'll keep our distance," I quickly added. "And if she starts to look tired, we'll leave immediately."

"I guess I can trust you with her," Mrs. Finberg said. "After all, you did save her life. But only for a few minutes."

Hope and I shared a smile as Mrs. Finberg got off the couch and took us back out to the foyer. I had been to Suze's house many times before. We didn't really need her mother to take us all the way upstairs, but she wasn't about to let us go unannounced . . . or without instructions.

Mrs. Finberg gently tapped on the door to Suze's bedroom. She spoke in a voice that I didn't think would even carry through the thin wood. "Suze, you have some visitors. Can we come in?"

"Yes, Mom," Suze said with a raspy voice. I immediately felt sorry for coming over. Hope hadn't said that Suze sounded so horrible when they had talked on the phone earlier. Even though I was curious about what had happened to her, I didn't want to totally impose.

At least when Mrs. Finberg opened the door Suze didn't

look as bad as she sounded. If anything, she actually looked pretty good for someone who had gone into anaphylactic shock the day before. She was sitting up in bed, but she didn't seem all that comfortable. Her head was kind of tilted back over the pile of pillows. It was like she had stuffed one too many of them behind her back.

Last time I was in Suze's bedroom must have been in the fifth grade, when we were making posters for her run for president of our elementary school. I was her campaign manager. We ran a great campaign, getting funny quotes from all my mom's famous clients to endorse Suze on the posters. Sadly, she lost the election. Holly Mayflower—Heather's sister—bought the vote with gift baskets from Snookie's Cookies.

Suze's bedroom hadn't changed much since then. It was a vision in lavender and lace. Imagine if an issue of *Martha Stewart Living* threw up and you'd only start to have an idea of what the room looked like.

"Hope, you didn't need to return the dress today," Suze squeaked out. She was almost lost in a sea of bedding and frills in her lavender and white canopy bed.

"Well, we both wanted to see you," Hope said. Her voice was oozing with concern.

"I told them they can only stay a few minutes," Suze's mom said from the doorway.

"Thank you," Suze replied with a slight cough. "But could you close the door? There's a draft."

"Sure, darling," Mrs. Finberg said.

As soon as the door shut behind Mrs. Finberg, Suze sat up straight and started pulling at the pillows behind her.

I rushed over to help. "Here, let me."

"That's okay," she said, waving me off. Her voice sounded perfectly normal. The raspy tone was gone.

Suze pulled a large sketchbook out from under her pillows. She opened it and checked the design I assume she had been working on when her mom knocked on the door. "I didn't have time to get this hidden comfortably," she said.

The sketch was pretty amazing. It was an updated version of Hope's dress. I couldn't believe that Suze had remembered so much detail from the small picture on Hope's cell phone screen, especially considering all that had happened right after Suze looked at it.

"You sure you can't make it back in time for the play?" Hope asked. "We could really use that kind of acting talent in the show. I honestly thought you were on death's door."

"Years of practice," Suze said. "Mom isn't happy unless I'm near terminal."

"But you *are* okay?" I asked.

"Fine," Suze said. "I could go back to school tomorrow, but you know Mom likes to keep an eye on me. It's actually funny this time, because of the show. She was all torn up, trying to decide if my starring role was worth risking my health. Ultimately, the hypochondria won out over the stage mothering. I think it's because I'm splitting the role with three other girls."

"Who knows if that will be true by the end of the week," I said.

The questioning look Suze gave me pretty much confirmed that no one—including Hope—had filled her in on the events of the day. I brought her up to speed, embellishing a few of the facts for dramatic effect. Hope didn't bother to correct me. She knows the healing properties of really good gossip. While I went through the story, Hope was busy taking the dress out of the garment bag and strategically hiding it in Suze's closet.

Since I knew I could trust Suze, I even filled her in on the part Cindy didn't want anyone to know. How could one possibly keep Victoria's Secret a secret? Especially from someone who needed cheering up.

"And I thought Cindy's bathing suit at the summer picnic was revealing," Suze said when I finished the tale.

"Oh, it was," I said, remembering back to the string bikini she had worn to the beach last June. "It was La Perla, don't you know?"

"I do, I do," Suze said, playing along. "Only Cindy would pay so much for so little material."

"Are we still on for shopping Sunday?" Hope asked. "I'd understand if you're not up to it."

"Oh, *I'm* up to it," Suze said. "I'm not sure my mom is. She's going to have to let me go to school on Monday if I'm going to pass finals. Maybe we can go sometime next week."

"Will that give you enough time before the prom?" Hope asked.

"Plenty," Suze replied. "I've already done my dress. Now I just need someone to go with." She looked at me. "I assume you're going with Sam?"

"Nope," I said.

"Oh, I thought . . ."

She wasn't the only one.

There was a soft tapping at the door. This time, Mrs. Finberg didn't bother to announce herself. Suze dropped her sketchbook on the floor and I helped out by pushing it under the bed with my foot.

"Just checking in," Mrs. Finberg said in a singsongy voice that subtly covered up the fact that she wanted us gone.

"A few more minutes, Mom?" Suze pled. "We haven't gone over my homework yet."

And I still hadn't asked what I wanted to know.

"One more minute," Mrs. Finberg said as she closed the door.

"We'll have to keep it quiet," Suze said softly. "She's waiting outside the door."

Seriously. There's overprotective and then there's *overprotective*. I can't imagine living with a parent who hovers like Suze's mom does. I bent down to retrieve the sketchbook from under the bed. It took me a second to find it, considering all that was going on down there.

"It's like this is the place where old sketchbooks go to die," I said as I pulled out the one I was pretty sure she had been working on.

"Yeah," Suze said with a resigned sigh. "I can't keep my sketchbooks out in the open. Mom prefers the performing arts over the visual ones. She keeps telling me how I deserve to be on the red carpet, not designing outfits for it."

Hope and I shook our heads. Having an incredibly talented daughter isn't enough for Mrs. Finberg. Suze has to be incredibly talented in the right way to make her mother happy.

Hope pulled Suze's books out of her bag. "Here's your homework—oops!" She dropped it all on the floor.

I bent to pick them up.

"That's okay," Hope said, pushing past me and nearly knocking me into Suze's nightstand. "Didn't you have something to ask Suze?"

Suze patted the bed for me to sit beside her.

"About the accident," I said as I sat.

"Accident?" Suze asked. "You really think it was an accident? The one person in the entire school who's allergic to shellfish just happened to get the one taco filled with shrimp?"

My thoughts exactly!

"So you think it was on purpose?" I asked.

"Don't you?" Suze said. "Isn't that why you're here?"

"Well, I'm here to make sure you're okay," I said quickly. "But yeah, that too. Any idea who had it in for you?"

"Half the cast," Suze said.

"Yeah, but none of them would want you dead," Hope said from the floor. She was taking an awful long time to pick up two schoolbooks and a few papers.

"Who said they thought I'd die?" Suze asked. "Everyone knows I carry the EpiPen. Besides, they probably figured the taco would make me break out in a huge rash like when that peanut M&M got mixed in with the regular ones at Mr. Whitman's Christmas party."

I had forgotten about that happening. The rash popped up within moments of her eating the peanut M&M. She had been in a green dress at the time. We all—including Suze—had joked at how the red rash was a perfect match for her Christmas dress. Suze's allergic reactions weren't always life threatening.

"Who could have switched out the tacos?" I asked. "Was anyone suspicious around your food?"

"Could've been," Suze said. "I was sitting with you guys for a while. And we were all distracted when Jax spilled that soda all over Sam."

"That's right!" I said. It was more than a simple coincidence that Heather's boyfriend had caused a commotion around the time that someone might have been replacing Suze's taco. Something was fishy, and it was Heather Mayflower who smelled like the mahimahi.

"All right," Mrs. Finberg said as she burst into the room. "Time to go. Suze needs her rest."

Hope quickly popped up from the floor and handed over the books. She was holding her garment bag closely to her chest.

"Thanks for coming by," Suze said as Mrs. Finberg quickly ushered us out of the bedroom.

Hope and I hurried downstairs, keeping ahead of Mrs. Finberg every step of the way. We quickly bypassed the living room, hoping Suze's mom wouldn't ask us to stay and talk more about Suze's fictional scene work. We managed to escape the house without further discussion.

"Crazy about that taco," I said to Hope as we walked to Electra. "Someone obviously must have planted it."

"It is a mystery, all right," Hope said as she opened the passenger side door.

"You know what's another mystery?" I asked as I got in the car.

"What?"

"Why you stole one of Suze's sketchbooks up there and hid it in your garment bag."

Hope looked at me with mock surprise. The look of glee on her face told me that she knew she'd been caught and she didn't care. "Yes," she said. "That is a mystery too."

Doubt

"Okay, Jimmy," Mr. Randall called offstage. "Let's see if this works."

"Just a second, Mr. Randall," Jimmy yelled back.

Poor Tasha looked nervous enough standing in the oversize basket. It was torture to make her wait any longer. I bet she never suspected that when she had been cast as the Wizard her life would ultimately be in the hands of Jimmy Wilkey.

"How you doing, Tasha?" I asked from my spot beside the basket. She forced a smile, but I could tell she was worried. I knew how she felt. If the contraption that Jimmy had rigged didn't work, that basket could fall off the platform and land on top of me.

After spending half the weekend checking out the light grid to make sure that none of the other clamps were rusted through, Jimmy and Mr. Randall had also re-rigged the fly system. They added a series of pulleys that could accommodate the basket of the "balloon" that would take the Wizard away from Oz. It was going to be the showstopping effect of the production. We expected it would even get its own applause.

If it could get up off the ground.

The Jordan Myers Fly System had been donated years ago to help lift set walls up above the stage for faster scene changes. We had never used it to lift anything with a person on it before. Thankfully, Jimmy's father asked one of the crew guys from the movie he was producing to help out with the rigging. There's no way the school would have let a student in the basket if Jimmy and Mr. Randall had been the only ones to work out the logistics.

The basket had already worked while it was empty. It had worked when we added books to simulate dead weight. But this was the first test with an actual person inside.

"Here we go," Jimmy said.

Tasha reached for the rim as the basket gave a little lurch. She was trying to look calm, but from where I stood I could tell she was shaking.

The basket lurched again, and then it started to rise straight up into the air. Slowly, it inched its way up off the platform. The movement was jerky at first, but the ride eventually smoothed out.

Tasha threw out her arms and looked out to the auditorium. "Second star to the right," she shouted, "and straight on till morning!"

It's not every day you see a girl with multiple piercings quoting Peter Pan while rising above a stage in an oversize wicker basket.

I *so* wish I had my camera at that moment.

To continue with the *Pan* homage for a moment: *She was flying. Flying!*

Tasha went right up into the rafters. She even stopped before she collided with the ceiling. Everyone in Hall Hall gave a cheer that was equal parts excitement and relief. It was the first thing that had gone right all week. Not bad considering it was still only Wednesday afternoon. Maybe we could get this show off the ground before Saturday.

"Good job, Jimmy," Mr. Randall yelled to the backstage area. "Bring her down!"

"Just a second!" Jimmy yelled back.

"Bryan," Mr. Randall said. "Can you go get Hope so we can run through the scene?"

"Sure," I said. I hopped off the stage and onto the house floor. I couldn't help but feel a twinge of optimism. Things were starting to look up. Literally.

Wednesday also marked the first day that nothing scandalous or life threatening had happened at lunch. Granted, Sam, Hope, and I had eaten with Anne in her classroom. Sam would have preferred to spend that time with Eric, but once I told her about my suspicions of Heather, she knew that being with her mom was the safer way to go. The pavilion and courtyard area had become a dangerous place for Dorothys this week.

With our three remaining Dorothys, we had split the afternoon rehearsal into three groups to maximize our time. Mr. Randall ran the technical blocking onstage, while Ms. Monroe handled musical numbers in the back of the auditorium and a third group worked on their own out in the lobby. From what I could tell, everything was starting to click.

"No, Heather," Ms. Monroe said in exasperation. "You can't bump fists with the Tin Woman. It's not correct for the time period."

I said, *starting* to click. I did not say *perfect*.

"What's wrong with updating this play a little?" Heather asked. "My dad has made a bundle updating old music with new talent. You could learn a thing or two from his business model."

"Even so—"

"Why don't we see what Mr. Randall says?" Heather didn't even wait for a reaction. She just stormed up the aisle.

Ms. Monroe looked at me as if I could do anything to help her with Heather.

I just shrugged. "I'm looking for Hope," I said.

"Outside," she said. I could tell Ms. Monroe wished she were outside as well.

I left the theater and went out to the foyer, where Hope and Sam were standing amid a group of ninth-grade munchkins.

"Hope, Mr. Randall needs to see you onstage," I said.

"But I'm working on my first entrance," Hope said.

"And he's working on your last entrance," I said. "Go figure."

Since flying the Wizard out had worked so well, Mr. Randall wanted to try flying Glinda in. Personally, I think he was being

Paul Ruditis

rather ambitious, but I didn't want to say anything about it. The poor guy had enough on his plate with this show. If he wanted to string up a few students, who was I to get in the way?

If only he had taken suggestions on which students to string up.

"You'd better go before someone offers to take your part," Sam said.

"Someone already has," I said. "Actually, three someones, so we should get back before we're both recast."

"Pretty soon we're going to run out of students," Sam joked.

No one laughed. Not even the munchkins.

Hope gave a dainty curtsy to Sam, which I assume meant she was still working on finding Glinda's character. Then she took my arm and went for the door.

"Bryan, wait a second," Sam said.

Hope and I both stopped. I suggested that she should go join the rehearsal. Mr. Randall could do without me for a minute. It's not like he was really in a position to start recasting the male roles now.

"What's up?" I asked.

Sam pulled me away from the group to stand over by the waterfall.

"I can't do a thing with the munchkins," she said in a whisper. The sound of the rushing water was a good cover for what she was saying.

"There's a sentence you don't hear every day," I said. "What's the sitch? Boozing and womanizing? I hear that was the problem with the original munchkins too."

"More like laziness and apathy," Sam said. "It's like they don't care."

"I guess I can't really blame them," I said. "Imagine you grow up around here with everyone talking about how great the Orion spring show is, then you finally get here and you're cast in this farce."

"Good point."

"Promise them that next year will be better. Then threaten them that Mr. Randall will remember how they all acted here when he casts next year's show."

"A little sugar and spice," Sam said. "I like it. How are things going in there?"

"Not horrible," I said. "Well, except for Heather."

"She hasn't tried anything?" Sam asked.

"Not yet," I said as I saw a very determined-looking Headmaster Collins storming our way. "But this looks promising."

The headmaster continued past us, heading into the auditorium. Anne was right behind him in full-teacher mode. She gave us this look that kind of said "Stay out of this," which made us so curious that we simply *had* to follow.

We weren't the only ones.

The munchkins were right on our heels.

Within moments, Headmaster Collins was leading a parade of our cast down the center aisle.

"Mr. Randall, I'm sorry, but I need to interrupt your rehearsal for a moment," Headmaster Collins said.

Mr. Randall looked out at the gaggle of students behind the headmaster and Sam's mom. He shook his head with resignation. "Headmaster Collins, I believe you already have."

"Be that as it may . . . Ms. Mayflower, may I speak with you for a moment?"

Heather looked around like he had been talking to someone else.

He wasn't.

"What is it?" she asked.

"Can you come down here?" Headmaster Collins said from the floor.

Heather did as she was asked and walked down to what would be the orchestra pit, if we had an orchestra.

"Can we take a look in your purse?" the headmaster asked.

Heather looked at Sam's mom, then back at the headmaster. "No."

"Ms. Mayflower," Headmaster Collins said with a measured calmness that I assume meant he knew Heather's father was out of the country at the moment.

Maybe he was meeting with my dad.

The headmaster continued: "We need to see the contents of your purse."

At this point, Anne noticed that pretty much the entire cast was leaning in to watch what was going on. "I think we should take this to your office, Headmaster Collins," she said quietly.

"This is ridiculous," Heather said, getting all dramatic for no apparent reason. She moved to the third row and grabbed her bag. "The play opens in three days. I don't have time for this." She handed her bag to the headmaster.

"Here. Don't blame me if you have to dig through feminine hygiene products."

Headmaster Collins's face went bright red. He held the purse out to Sam's mom. She didn't take it. "I'm uncomfortable going through a student's personal possessions," she said. I didn't blame her. She knows a potential lawsuit when she sees one. With Suze and the shrimp taco, that could be two lawsuits in one week.

That doesn't come close to the record around here, though.

"Fine." Heather grabbed the bag and walked over to the stage.

She began pulling out the contents. I couldn't quite make out everything that she was holding, but it was clear when she got to the bottom of the bag that there was something there that surprised her. She quickly closed the bag.

The headmaster held out his hand. "Ms. Mayflower."

She handed over the bag. "I don't know how that got in there."

Headmaster Collins opened the bag and pulled out a CD. He showed the CD to Anne, who nodded her head.

"Ms. Mayflower, we now need to go to the office," the headmaster said. "Mr. Randall, I think you should come along as well."

"Headmaster, we really do need to be rehearsing for the show right now," Mr. Randall said.

"This won't take long," Headmaster Collins said. "And the show is involved as well."

It was clear that Mr. Randall did not like the sound of that. "Let's hold off on flying Hope for the moment."

"How 'bout we cancel that idea altogether?" Hope asked. Did I mention she has a thing about heights?

Mr. Randall ignored her and kept giving out instructions. "Ms. Monroe, please continue with your group. Sam, take your people back out to the lobby and work the opening. And . . . Bryan, can you go over the ending onstage for me?"

"Sure," I said.

Like there was a chance any of us were going to be doing any work while he was gone.

Once the doors to the theater shut behind Headmaster Collins, Anne, Mr. Randall, and Heather, the cast broke out in numerous conversations at once. Poor Ms. Monroe didn't even have a chance at maintaining control. Eventually she gave in and gossiped along with the rest of us.

The cast spent the next fifteen minutes trying to figure out what that had been all about. Most people thought Headmaster Collins had pulled out a copy of the CD containing the nude photos of Cynthia. But that didn't explain why Sam's mom was involved.

The conspiracy theorists in the group suggested that it could be a CD containing a secret school budget that Headmaster Collins didn't want anyone to see for legal reasons. Most of us ignored them. They're the same ones who insist FOX rigs the voting on *American Idol* to provide them with the most marketable stars.

There were several other theories floating around the room,

but none of them sounded plausible to me. Sam was the only one not offering a suggestion. I think she was thinking about how Heather's departure could affect her. If Heather was out of the play, then we definitely had a chance to salvage the show. But that would only leave two Dorothys, and with three days before curtain, anything could happen.

Once Mr. Randall got back, we heard the full story.

"Heather is no longer in the play," he confirmed our suspicions without bothering to brace us for the news.

Hope was the first to regain her voice. "People come and go so quickly here."

Nervous laughter filled the auditorium.

"She was found in possession of Ms. Lawson's final exam," he continued.

"She took the test?" Jason asked.

"Heather claims that she is innocent," Mr. Randall said. "She said someone planted it there."

"Was she expelled?" a munchkin asked.

"No," Mr. Randall said in his most official, "Don't gossip with me" tone. "Since the headmaster could not immediately disprove her claim, he could not take such drastic action."

"But he could kick her out of the play," Sam said.

"Extracurricular activities are discretionary," Mr. Randall said. "Now, that's all we're going to say on the subject. We have a lot of work to do. Sam, you're still going to be Dorothy for act one. Wren, you've now got the entire second act."

At that announcement, several girls converged on Mr. Randall to repeat what they had been putting him through since Monday. Like there was really time to keep shifting roles in the next two days.

"So much for your theory on Heather being behind Suze and Cindy getting kicked out of the play," Hope said.

"I haven't changed my mind," I said.

"But she's not in the play anymore either," Sam said, not sounding all that disappointed.

"This is *Heather*," I reminded them. "The girl who, in one phone call, got The Pussycat Dolls, John Mayer, and Shakira to perform at the fall dance for free." And the call wasn't even to her dad. "She's up to something."

Neither Sam nor Hope said anything. I wasn't sure if they agreed with me or thought I was crazy. But I had known Heather long enough not to underestimate the girl. She was behind all this. I just couldn't figure out this latest stunt.

But, more importantly, I was worried. There were only two Dorothys left. One of them was my best friend. So far we had gone through near death, total embarrassment, and possible expulsion. This was serious whether or not Heather was behind it.

Oh, but Heather was behind it.

Of that, I had no doubt.

Just because she was caught up in her little plan didn't mean she wasn't the one pulling the strings. Heather's pretty good at this manipulation thing. She's had a lot of practice. I didn't count her out yet.

Now, gentle reader, before you go thinking I'm all paranoid and suspicious for no reason, let me make one thing very clear: As far as I'm concerned, there's no mystery in this mystery. There isn't going to be one of those meaningful life lessons with a heavy-handed moral on making assumptions about people. This is the real world . . . or as real as it can get in Malibu. Things are pretty much the way they look around here.

Simply put: Heather is evil.

And I'm going to prove it.

The Rivals

Since the rehearsal had already run longer than usual, Mr. Randall dismissed everyone but the two remaining Dorothys. I guess he wanted Sam to work with Wren since she was now performing all of act two. He also asked Hope to stick around to see if they could try to work out the rigging on her, bringing new meaning to the phrase, "High Hopes."

This meant that I was free to go. But since I had nothing better to do, I was planning on sticking around to watch . . . until Sam came up to me with a look in her eyes that clearly spelled trouble with a capital T, and that rhymes with E, and that stands for . . . you can see where this is going.

"Can you *please* do me a favor and tell Eric I can't make our date?" Sam asked. They were supposed to go out to dinner together. On a school night, no less. Has that boy learned anything about asking a girl out yet?

"He'll figure it out eventually," I said. "You know. When you don't show up and all."

"Bryan!"

"You do realize this is the second time in one week that I've had to walk all the way over to the soccer field because of you," I said.

Sam pushed out her bottom lip in a pout. She wasn't playing the girl card, she was making fun of me. "Poor baby. Besides, they'll be back in the locker room by now. No need to risk fresh air and exercise."

"In that case," I said, then turned and walked away.

"Thank you!" she called after me.

I waved back at her over my shoulder, successfully managing not to storm off like a spoiled four-year-old. This is the problem with not having cell phones at school. When Mr. Randall decided to call that extended rehearsal, Sam had no artificial means to blow off Eric.

She needed me to do it for her.

Normally, I'd have no problem with telling Eric that Sam had to bail on him. Heck, it could probably even be fun. But there was nothing enjoyable about doing it in front of the soccer team.

First of all, there was the locker room. I've never felt particularly welcome in the locker room. Not for the reason you think, either. I'm not afraid of the locker rooms or anything. It's kind of like the school dressing room. I'm sure the soccer guys wouldn't feel comfortable in the dressing room either.

Like I said earlier, we don't have defined cliques. There's a lot of overlap. The jocks are brains and all that. But there are two groups that simply don't mesh: the soccer team and the Drama Geeks. Or, I should say, the soccer team and the *male* Drama Geeks. More and more of the girls in drama seem to be dating soccer players these days.

It's not that the personalities don't click. It's not that one group of guys thinks it's better than the other. It's just that the spring show rehearses all during soccer season. Girls can play volleyball or swim in the fall and winter. Guys can swim too, if they want. But the only things that really overlap are soccer and the spring show. That means the choice is one or the other for guys. You're either in the show or on the soccer team.

That's why I was standing outside the locker room waiting for my best friend's new boyfriend instead of going in and finding him. Well, maybe it was because of that other reason a bit too. I never quite know where to look when I'm in a locker room. All those guys in various states of undress. At the same time, I don't want to look like I'm not looking. But then I don't want to overcompensate by looking too much so it doesn't look like I'm not trying to look when all I want to do is *really* look.

You know what I mean?

Thankfully, I didn't have to wait long out in the hall. Jax was the first guy to come out of the locker room. "Yo, Stark. What are you doing hanging around the locker room?"

So many answers came to mind at that moment. Obviously, I couldn't use the actual reason. Saying "I'm here to break a date for Sam" probably wouldn't go over too well.

Didn't want to go messing up my street cred by looking like anybody's errand boy.

What? Stop laughing.

Lacking a better plan, I simply changed the subject.

"Uh . . . Jax, have you heard about Heather?"

"What happened now?" he asked with an exasperated sigh that wasn't nearly as impressive as his girlfriend's abilities in that area.

I quickly filled him in on the latest news. Even though I didn't have much to say, I'm pretty sure it was the longest conversation that he and I had ever had. By the time I reached the end of the tale, Jax looked even more shocked than Heather had.

"How did that test get in her bag?" he asked.

"Beats me."

"The headmaster doesn't really think she'd cheat, does he?"

"I don't know."

"Is she still here?"

This time, I just shrugged. "I honestly don't know anything more than what I told you."

I guess he found my lack of information annoying, because he bolted down the hall without another word. I assume he was going to the headmaster's office. I couldn't begin to imagine what he was going to do once he got there.

Slowly the rest of the team filed out in dribs and drabs. Most of the guys said, "Hey, Stark," and kept walking.

No one snubbed me.

No one stopped to hang out with me either.

Finally, Eric came out, along with Drew.

"See," he said to Drew, "you can't hold back on the field. You see a guy coming at you, don't flinch, don't slow down. Just keep barreling. . . ." He trailed off when he saw me waiting.

"Are you in the wrong place?" Drew asked.

"Undoubtedly," I said, then turned my attention to Eric. "Sam has to cancel on your date tonight."

Eric quickly covered up a look of what could have been disappointment. Even more quickly, he adopted what could have been described as a macho posturing attitude. "And she couldn't tell me herself?"

After a quick roll of the eyes, I filled him in on the latest school gossip and how it affected Sam and, by default, him.

"Can't she go out after?" he asked.

"Not on a school night," I said, sounding exactly like I knew Anne would.

"Can you ask her?"

"Do I *look* like a messenger service?"

"Actually, yes," Drew chimed in unnecessarily.

"Was I *asking* you?"

"Nope," he said. "Just saying."

"Dude," Eric said to me. "What's your problem?"

"I don't have a problem," I lied.

"Do you like Sam?" Eric asked. "'Cause if you do, you need to take it up with her."

What an idiot. "I am *not* interested in Sam," I said with complete and total honesty. "Why would you even think something like that?"

"Because you've been on my case since I asked her out."

I wasn't quite sure how to answer that. Other than Sam and Hope, people don't often call me on things.

Luckily, Drew came to my rescue.

"Dude," he said to Eric. (Again with the "dude.") "That's not true. Bryan's been on your case since long before you ever went for Sam."

My hero.

Not.

"You're right," Eric said. "Why is that? Jealous of my good looks and natural athletic ability?"

Again, my eyes did a roll. Like he didn't know why I couldn't stand him. But we weren't here for that conversation. "That must be it," I said. "Now, if you'll excuse me, I've got to get back to rehearsal."

"Hey," Eric said as I started to walk off.

"What?"

"Seriously. Can you ask her to call me when she gets home?"

"Fine," I said as I continued walking.

I didn't really have to get back to rehearsal. All I was going to do was sit around. I could have gone home, but all I'd do is sit around there, too. At least at the rehearsal I'd be able to keep an eye on Sam in case any other mishaps happened.

When I got back in the theater, Hope was yelling at Jimmy because the rigging had ripped her shirt. At this point there wasn't a doubt in my mind that Mr. Randall's dream about having Glinda the Good Witch float in and out of the play was not going to come to pass.

While Hope abused our poor, defenseless stage manager, I pulled Sam aside to pass along Eric's message. I briefly toyed with forgetting to tell her that he had asked her to call later, but I figured that was pointless. She'd eventually find out about it.

Then she'd be all "Why didn't you tell me?" and stuff.

Then I'd have to defend myself.

Then we'd get into a fight.

No . . . if I was going to sabotage this thing between her and Eric, I'd have to be much sneakier about it than that.

But first, we had to get through the play. I wasn't about to try anything with Sam's life—or at least her role—potentially in danger. There were only two more rehearsals to get through before we were in the clear.

The scary part was that one of those rehearsals—tomorrow's, in fact—was our all-day tech rehearsal. That meant a whole school day fraught with potential danger for the remaining Dorothys.

And I still wasn't entirely off book yet.

The Taming of the Shrew

What can I say about the All-Day Rehearsal?

You know how everyone says that the band continued to play as the *Titanic* sank? Well, the all-day rehearsal was kind of like that. First the "wind machine"—which was nothing more than a couple fans we "borrowed" from the computer lab—couldn't even create enough wind to blow a piece of paper across the stage. Then, Jason got stuck on the Scarecrow's post and couldn't get down. But the highlight had to be when Gary McNulty got a little too *into* his part as the lead flying monkey and took a header off the stage. He was okay, but we had to stop the rehearsal while the nurse checked him out and gave him a couple faculty-approved aspirin.

But, through it all, the band sounded great! That wasn't much of a surprise, since we only used prerecorded music for the show. At least the music was clear as it came out of Mr. Randall's iPod and was piped through the auditorium's sound system.

The rehearsal ran to the end of the school day. We all wanted to stay longer, but Mr. Randall had said that we'd done enough. Actually, he said that he'd *had* enough, but . . . same thing.

Tired and dejected, we all took seats so Mr. Randall could go over notes with us and tell us everything we did wrong. That took about a half hour. The past few days of rehearsals had been so focused on the Dorothy drama that we'd hardly been able to work on the rest of the play. So, *everyone* got notes.

The munchkins were stepping all over one another's lines.

The Tin Woodspeople were having makeup issues.

And *everyone* needed to find the light at one time or another.

It went on for a while. We got notes as groups and as individuals. Hope was still having problems settling on her motivations for Glinda. I dropped a few lines that were kind of important to the plot. Sam got surprisingly few notes considering that most of her part was new. In fact, she got the least notes of anyone in the show.

The same could not be said about Dorothy #2. Nobody could really blame Wren. She'd only had the part for three days. I'm sure Mr. Randall was considering giving the entire role to Sam, but there was no way in the world—or at least in the world of Orion Academy—that he could do that and still keep his job.

Once the notes were done, I guess Mr. Randall figured it was time for the old inspirational speech to the saddest group of actors I'd ever seen. You know the speech: the old, "You want fame? Well, fame costs." That kind of thing.

I don't know if it was intentional or if Jimmy was just

working on the sound system, but throughout Mr. Randall's monologue the prerecorded "band" was playing "The Merry Old Land of Oz."

Ironic, no?

"Listen, guys," Mr. Randall said, gearing up for his load of inspiration. "I know this week has been tough. I know you've all put in a tremendous amount of work on a show that—let's be honest—none of us wanted to do in the first place." Not quite the Saint Crispin's Day speech from Shakespeare's *Henry V* (*Aside:* Act IV, Scene iii), but the guy did have a rough day. "And I know that you're all scared about the show opening in two days." The music began to crescendo. "I'm scared too. But in the history of theater there have been more daunting obstacles to overcome. Think of the time when plays were outlawed and actors could be arrested for doing nothing more than setting foot on a stage." He was shouting over the music. "Dare I say it, but the show must go on!"

At this point the music was blaring so loudly that half of us were covering our ears.

"Jimmy!" Mr. Randall shouted. "Can you *please* turn that down?"

"I'm sorry, Mr. Randall," Jimmy yelled from the soundboard at the back of the auditorium. "But something's wrong with the sound system. I'm dancing as fast as I can."

At least, that's what it sounded like he said. Upon further reflection it was probably, "I'm doing the best that I can." Then again, with Jimmy, you never really can tell. Besides, the music was so loud that no one could hear him, anyway.

"Everyone go home," Mr. Randall finally said as the band played on.

Most of the cast took their cue and fled the theater as the music blared. I could tell that it was really getting to Sam, because she was out of there without so much as a "good-bye." Which is kind of rude, if you ask me.

"Need a ride home?" I yelled at Hope as she gathered her things. Those things included a flat cardboard box about the size of the sketchbook that Hope had taken from Suze's room the other day. I would have asked her what she was doing with it, but I was pretty sure she wouldn't tell me, so why bother?

"That's okay," she said. "I'm getting a ride with the steps. They're helping me out with . . . an errand."

"What's that costing you?"

"My dignity," she replied before bolting out of the auditorium.

She wasn't kidding. Since Alexis and Belinda were the primary car drivers—and the car was purchased during Hope's time abroad—the double-mental twins got to decide what car to buy. Their choice? A pink and purple Mini Cooper. A *customized* pink and purple Mini Cooper with a silver diamond etched on the roof, sparkly pink spinners on the wheels, and purple fur covered seats.

In some ways the car sounds like it could be really cool. Trust me. It's not.

Within moments, the only people left in the theater were Jimmy, Mr. Randall, Wren, and me. Wren was trying to talk to Mr. Randall, but it was clear that they were having trouble hearing each other over the blasting music. Finally, Mr. Randall left the auditorium, after motioning wildly for Wren to have a seat and wait for him. Me? I should have left when I had the chance.

As I gathered my books, I felt a tap on my shoulder. When I turned, Jimmy was behind me. "A little help?" he yelled over the still blaring music.

"Why don't you unplug the iPod?" I asked back.

He yelled something about still needing to fix the sound system. I'm not entirely sure what he said because he did ramble on about it for a while. It was pretty hard to hear, even if I *had* been trying to listen.

"What do you need?" I finally asked.

After a few false starts, Jimmy finally managed to indicate that he wanted me to stand onstage while he played with the sound system. If he ever managed to get the sound back to something approaching normal in the auditorium, I could tell him how it sounded onstage. That way, he wouldn't have to run all over the theater to check the sound levels. Having nothing better to do for the second day in a row, I agreed and took a spot onstage.

Jimmy managed to get the music down a couple notches on the stage speakers. I tried to tell him that, but he wasn't looking up from the soundboard. After about a minute of waving wildly at him, I gave up. Wren was starting to look at me funny. You'd think she'd get out of her seat and go tell him. Ultimately it didn't matter because the sound went right back up to deafening.

While we worked I saw the red light on the cordless stage phone light up. Mr. Randall had left it with his stuff in the front row. The phone usually stays in its base backstage, constantly in silent mode in case anyone needs to call during a performance. The blinking light grabbed Wren's attention as well. Since she was the closest, she got up to answer it. As one would expect, the conversation must have been difficult. Eventually, she hung up and left the auditorium, leaving me alone to contemplate my inner munchkin.

After about five more minutes of an endless loop of "The Merry Old Land of Oz" I was starting to get rather bored. I looked over at the side of the stage and saw the Wicked Witch of the East's backup legs propped up against Dorothy's house. Jimmy being Jimmy, he had an extra pair of mannequin legs ready to be placed under the house in case something happened to the original pair. Between multiple legs, multiple Totos, and multiple cast members, it was beginning to look like we were performing our play on Noah's Ark. Then again, considering how some people thought the play was cursed, I wouldn't have been surprised if a flash flood had come bursting through the theater at any moment.

Since I was effectively alone, I decided to have some fun. I pulled the legs out onstage with me and danced them around to the music. We started out with a little tap and then moved into a few ballet moves for variety and then hit up a kick line. I was really starting to get into it too, when the music suddenly cut out.

"Peace, at last," I said into the silent auditorium, and I put the legs to rest.

"Mr. Randall!" a shrill voice bellowed from behind me. One

of the backstage doors slammed open revealing a very angry Heather Mayflower, heading straight for me. "Where is Mr. Randall?" she demanded.

"I don't know," I said. I looked out to Jimmy for help, but he had ducked under the soundboard again. I couldn't tell if he was working on the system or hiding. My bet was on hiding.

"Is he coming back?"

"He left his stuff." I pointed to the front row.

Heather stared at me like she was waiting for something. It was rather uncomfortable. "He could be in his office," I suggested.

"I stopped there first," Heather said.

I looked to the back of the auditorium. Jimmy was still under the soundboard. At that point, I figured it was either him or me. "Maybe Jimmy knows. He's back there working on the soundboard."

I guess my voice carried, because Jimmy's head suddenly popped up. I couldn't tell for sure from the distance, but I could swear he was glaring at me angrily.

"Jimmy!" Heather shrieked as she left the stage and walked up the aisle.

I watched for a minute while Heather accosted Jimmy. The poor guy was trapped behind the soundboard. I couldn't hear what Heather was going on about, but I could tell that Jimmy wasn't able to get a word in.

Logic told me I should stay right where I was. I had successfully pawned Heather off to the stage manager. He would deal with her. That was his job, after all. If only I hadn't been born so naturally curious. Before I knew it, my feet were taking me up the aisle because my ears were wondering what Heather was in such a snit about. If only my body had listened to my brain. By the time I reached Heather and Jimmy, the sound system had mysteriously burst back on again and music was blaring throughout the auditorium.

"Jimmy!" Heather yelled over the music.

He did his best to ignore her while he fumbled with the wiring. "I have to fix this," he shouted back. "Talk to Bryan!"

My body went numb. He was throwing me to the wolf.

I wanted to yell, *Traitor!* But, quite frankly, he was only returning the favor. I had sold him out first.

"You can talk to Randall for me," Heather said as she grabbed my arm. Roughly. "Tell him to put me back in the show. He'll listen to you."

"I don't think it's Mr. Randall's decis—"

Heather wasn't interested in logic. "If I get enough teachers on my side, we can all go to Headmaster Collins."

"I don't know," I said. "Jimmy should—"

I didn't think it was possible, but the music got even louder. With an annoyed glance Jimmy's direction, Heather proceeded to pull me out of the auditorium to continue our conversation. Why hadn't I gone home when I had the chance?

"Please tell me you'll talk to Randall," Heather said, once we were in the silence of the hallway. I swear I heard the music cut out a split second before the auditorium door closed.

I couldn't imagine what Heather expected me to say to Mr. Randall. The school took a pretty harsh stance on cheating. If it was any other student—that is, any other student with a different father—she would have been suspended. Personally, I was surprised she was even having this discussion with me. With a father like hers, I wouldn't have been enlisting students to help me. Particularly students I could barely even consider a friend. I'd go straight to Daddy.

"My dad's in New York with Holly," Heather said, as if she knew what I was thinking. Now, there's a scary thought: a psychic Heather Mayflower.

Psychotic? Definitely.

"Can't you call him?" I asked.

"And tell him I was kicked out of the show for cheating on a test?" Heather was nearly hyperventilating. "He'd tell me I deserved it and hang up. But first he'd tell me not to bother him while he was working on Holly's career. You heard her show got picked up, right?"

Actually, I hadn't. Holly was in New York for upfronts. That was when all the TV networks decided their schedules for the fall season. It looked like Holly was going to be starring in a new sitcom come fall. The thought of senior year free of Mayflowers brought a smile to my face that I hoped Heather read as happiness for her sister. "That's great!"

That's when the tears started flowing. "No, it's not!" Heather screeched. Mrs. Brown stopped in the hallway to look at us. Once she saw who was doing the screeching, she continued on, not wanting to get involved. I couldn't blame her.

Scratch that. I could blame her. And I do.

"Just one more thing Holly's better at than me," Heather whined. "She's my *little* sister. Do you know how much that sucks?"

Considering that they were only a year apart, it was hard to think of Holly as all that much "littler." Besides, she's half a foot taller than Heather, anyway. Not having any siblings of my own, though, I couldn't really imagine what Heather was going through. Or why she was being so melodramatic about it.

She grabbed my hand and held it in both of hers. "Promise me you'll talk to Mr. Randall," she hissed.

At this point, she was starting to freak me out. "What do you want me to say?"

"That someone put that test in my bag," she said as if it were the most logical thing in the world. "Remind him that I'm going to be class valedictorian. I don't need to cheat on a test."

She had a good point there. Heather may be lacking a heart, but the girl has more than her fair share in the brains department. As many enemies as she has, I couldn't imagine anyone risking suspension to pull that kind of prank. Especially since it was guaranteed that Heather wouldn't get more than a slap on the wrists. Still, it did get her kicked out of the show, so it wouldn't have been a worthless prank.

I still firmly believed that Heather was the one behind Suze and Cindy finding their way out of the show. I just couldn't figure out how this fit into her plan. And then it came to me: She'd intended to plant the test on Wren, but was caught before she could do it.

Hoisted on her own petard, as they say. Okay, I don't know who really says that. But it's such a great way to say that she fell into her own trap.

"Besides, who wants to see Wren try to act? She has no talent."

Somewhere a pot was in the process of calling a kettle black. "And, I know Sam's your friend and all, but she only goes here because her mom's a teacher."

I didn't really see what that had to do with anything. Nor did I see how she thought attacking my best friend was going to bring me around to her side. I stood there in silence because it was clear that I wasn't her scene partner. I was her audience.

As usual.

"I need to be in this show," Heather cried to me. For the briefest moment I could have sworn I saw something approaching a genuine emotion, but it was hastily covered by her histrionics. "It will show my father that I'm just as good as Holly. I know I shouldn't be so petty. But you don't know my father. You don't know how hard I try. Bryan, we've been friends for years and years." *We have?* "You've got to talk to Mr. Randall for me. You will, right? Promise me!" She ended her monologue by collapsing on my shoulder with heaving sobs.

Wow. That was . . . wow.

"Promisssse!"

"I promise," I said, not meaning it at all.

As I stood there, patting her overly processed hair, I was certain of one thing: Heather really was a horrible actress.

Okay, two things: Someone needed a trip to the stylist because her roots were totally starting to show.

Witness for the Prosecution

The thing about a good lie is that it should always be based in some form of the truth. That way, you can always justify it to yourself as being *partially* true and therefore not a *total* lie. At the very least, it makes it easier for you to recall some part of the story if you ever get questioned about it later.

I had no doubt that Heather's underlying story was true. She *was* jealous of her younger, more talented, and—let's be honest—more beautiful sister. That wasn't much of a surprise. Heather may be fairly hot and even more intelligent, but Holly is the star in the family. At least that part of Heather's "breakdown" rang true—overwrought and melodramatic, but true. The real question was why the heck was she telling *me?*

It took me a few minutes to extricate myself from Heather's clutches. I could have gone back into the theater, but I had nothing more to say to Jimmy. He had thrown me to the proverbial lioness, with a smile on his face.

Well, I couldn't swear to the smile, but I suspect it was there after we had left the auditorium. Either way, he wasn't getting any more help from me. Instead, I went to my locker, picked up my things, and headed for home.

As soon as I was in a cell friendly area—my driveway—I tried calling Sam to tell her all about Lady Heather and her theatrics. No one was home at Sam's house, and she's cell free no matter what area she's in, so I was thwarted in my effort to gossip. All I could do was go into my house and wait. And patience is *so* not a virtue of mine.

I went in through the kitchen, hung up my fedora, and didn't bother to call out to tell anyone that I was home. Mom was still at the bow-wow-tique (her word, not mine) and Dad was in some foreign country below the equator, if I remember correctly.

I grabbed a cherry Pop-Tart and pulled up a leather and steel stool to sit at the stainless-steel island in our stainless-steel kitchen. Aside from my room, the kitchen is the only room in the house I'm ever comfortable in. It's sleek and cool and totally to my father's specifications. He's an amazing cook, and the room is the one place that's totally his when he's in country. The rest of the house belongs to Mom.

Dad and I call the rest of the house "the Museum" because of its perfect preservation. My room and the kitchen are the only two rooms where you're allowed to wear shoes. Or drink anything that could stain. Or collect dust.

I pulled out my script so I could run lines while I snacked. The show was in two days. We might not have any Dorothys by then, but I'd be damned if I was going to drop a line.

I read the lines aloud, hoping that reading them and hearing them would count twice toward memorizing them. Hey, it was worth a shot. I'd sleep with the script under my pillow if I thought I could memorize through osmosis.

I managed to get all the way through my act when the doorbell started blowing up.

Not bothering to clean up my plate, I raced to the foyer worried that the world was coming to the end. As the bell continued to ring, I threw open the door to find Sam in a highly agitated state.

"I need you as an alibi," Sam said.

"Gladly," I replied, ushering her into the house. "For what?"

"You haven't heard?"

"Hence the question."

Sam slipped off her shoes and plopped down on Mom's white leather couch in the media room. She tucked her feet in beneath her, trying to get comfortable, but still looking rather manic. "Wren had an accident. She's out of the show."

"Is she okay?"

"Sprained her ankle."

"What? Where? How?"

"Attacked. Observatory. Sabotage."

"Tell."

"From what Jimmy told me," she said, "Wren got this call while the sound system was still malfunctioning."

"I saw that," I said, realizing that I was a small part of the story. "I don't know how she heard anyone on the phone over the music, but she left the auditorium after she hung up."

"Whoever called her pretended to be Mr. Randall," Sam explained. "The person told her to meet him—or her—in the observatory so they could rehearse the jitterbug number."

"In the observatory?"

"They needed a large enough space," Sam continued.

"And Jimmy and I were still working on the sound system in the auditorium," I said.

"Right," Sam noted. "But when she got to the observatory, Mr. Randall wasn't there."

"Please don't tell me she went inside," I begged.

Sam nodded.

I shook my head. Wren was usually smarter than that. Dorothys were dropping faster than flying monkeys in a field of poppies. Why in the world would she go into the observatory because a mysterious voice on the phone told her to?

"She said she heard a noise," Sam explained. "From behind the telescope. Like someone was hurt."

"And she couldn't go and get help?"

"She wasn't sure what it was," Sam said. "So she went to check."

"And she was attacked?"

"Not exactly. You know how the only way to get around the telescope is up on the catwalk?"

"Oh, no," I said, anticipating where this was going. The telescope in the observatory is pretty huge. To look through the telescope, you have to walk up a small metal staircase onto a catwalk about five feet off the ground. That's the only way you can get to the other side of the telescope too.

"She made it to the top step and the tread came loose," Sam explained. "She fell down the steps, backward. Then, the lights went out. She heard someone drop from the catwalk in the dark and saw a body run out the door, but she couldn't tell who it was."

"Is she okay?"

"Just a few bruises," Sam said. "And the sprain."

"Wren can still do the show with a sprained ankle."

"She's a dancer, not an actress," Sam said.

"But she's a pretty good actress," I insisted.

"Doesn't matter to her," Sam clarified. "If she can't do the jitterbug, she doesn't want to do the show. She doesn't even want to go back to being a Glinda."

"Leaving you as the lone Dorothy," I stated the obvious. Then I got a little more obvious. "Until someone decides you were the one behind all the attacks."

"See why I need an alibi?" she asked.

"Actually, no," I said, stalling. I didn't want to tell her what horrible thought just popped into my head. I played a bigger part in this story than I'd originally thought. "What were you doing during the attack?"

"I was alone."

Notice how that wasn't the answer to the question I had asked. It was an answer, yes, but not the one required. "Were you still at school?" I hoped I could back into the truth here.

"Yes."

"Waiting for your mom?"

"No," Sam said. "But that's not important. I need you to say you were with me if anyone asks."

"But you won't tell me what you were doing?"

"I said it's not important," Sam reiterated, which only made it even more important for me to know the truth. "I need your help. You were right all along. Heather's got to be behind this. She'll be coming for me next, and I need to protect myself. And the first thing I have to do is stop her from pinning Wren's attack on me."

"*That's* why she was caught with the test," I said. "Because now she's not a suspect."

"But she's still not in the play."

"I'm sure she's got that covered."

"Which is why I need an alibi."

Which is why she should tell me what she was really doing. And just so you don't go thinking the wrong thing, there wasn't a doubt in my mind that Sam was innocent. She would never hurt anyone over a part. Okay, maybe she would for the *right* part, but not for Dorothy in the Orion Academy Spring Theatrical Production of *The Wizard of Oz*.

As our conversation had already started going in circles, I figured it was time to drop my bombshell. "I can't be your alibi," I said. "I was with Heather when Wren was attacked. Jimmy and Mrs. Brown saw me."

"She could have had an accomplice," Sam suggested. "Heather would never get her hands dirty."

"I don't doubt that," I said. "But it doesn't help you with your alibi problem. What about Hope?"

"She was with the steps," Sam said. "And there's no way we'd get them to lie about being with me, too. They're Holly's best friends. They would never turn on their best friend's sister like that."

"I don't know about that," I said, thinking back to Heather's hatred for her sister. Odds are the feeling was mutual, I'm sure. But we couldn't risk it. Alexis and Belinda want nothing more out of life than to be "sources close to the celebrity" when they grow up. You know the ones. They are the "friends" who run to the tabloids when their close celebrity "friend" is contemplating divorce, or has just found out she's pregnant, or has switched to decaf. Which is just my way of saying they love a good scandal more than the average Malibu teen. And that was saying something.

I had a possible solution to Sam's problem, but I wasn't willing to use it and was hoping to come up with another.

None came.

"What about Eric?" I asked.

"He's on his way to LAX," Sam explained. "He and Drew are meeting with the soccer recruiter for the University of New Mexico tomorrow. I guess they have one of the best soccer programs in the country."

"Really? I get the Eric part, but Drew really thinks he's that good?"

"Bryan! Focus!"

"Sorry," I said, getting back on task. "But why can't you say you were with Eric at the time? Wasn't that, like, over an hour ago?"

"Because he's not here to back me up," Sam said.

"What? He doesn't have a cell phone?" I didn't like the direction this conversation was taking.

"There was soccer practice this afternoon."

Now I knew I didn't like where this was going. Notice she didn't say, "He was *at* soccer practice this afternoon."

"He didn't go to practice today," I said, filling in the blank.

Sam looked down at the couch. Since there was nothing there to look at but white leather, I'm guessing she was trying to avoid my piercing stare. "I felt bad about canceling our date yesterday," she said. "And with him going away the next few days . . . we wanted to spend some time together."

Oh, how *cute*. Blech. But I had other things on my mind at the moment. I did a quick check to confirm she was still wearing her unicorn necklace. See, Sam has this thing about unicorns. In mythology, unicorns only approach girls who are still pure (meaning: virgins). Sam had confided in me long ago that when she finally loses her pure status she would take off the necklace once and for all.

It was still on her.

But that didn't really have anything to do with the issue at hand.

"This isn't the fifties. You don't have to worry about your virtue being intact." Though I was glad to see that it was. "So what? You and Eric were locking lips at the time."

Sam shook her head. "The soccer team isn't allowed to miss practice without an excuse," Sam said. "Eric told Coach Zach he had to leave early so he could get his medical files for the recruiter. If the coach finds out Eric was with me, he'll be suspended from the finals."

"And the world as we know it will come to an end," I said.

"Bryan!"

"How about this scenario: Headmaster Collins thinks that you're behind the disappearing Dorothys and expels you."

"There's nothing that points to me in this," she said, backpedaling.

"Except that you're the last Dorothy standing," I reminded her. "Even if people don't start suspecting you, you should start worrying about what could happen to you next."

"I can protect myself," she said.

"I don't doubt that," I said. "But Heather's out to stop the Dorothys. And I'm pretty sure she's got one more move in her to take you out of the play and get herself back in. You need to protect yourself. You need to call Eric."

Sam had come to me looking for an alibi. Why was she suddenly more concerned about her relationship with Eric?

"Okay," she said, leading me to false hope. "I'll call Eric . . . if I have to."

"News flash, Sam: You *have* to! Heather will be out for you next."

"Do you always have to be so dramatic?"

"Excuse me? You're the one who freaks out over how every little quiz affects your GPA. And now you're not even worried about being expelled? Not to mention criminal charges. We're talking about two attacks here."

"I see what you're saying," Sam said as she got off the couch and moved to the foyer. "But it'll all be fine. Trust me."

"You, I trust. It's Heather who worries me."

"I'll be careful," Sam said as she slipped into her sandals.

I wanted to say, "It doesn't matter how careful you are." I wanted to tell her she was totally insane. I wanted to say, "Why are you leaving so soon? You just got here." But I knew she wouldn't hear me.

She had Eric on the brain.

Which, believe me, is as disgusting as it sounds.

And Then There Were None

Friday morning started out with a different energy from the rest of the week. It's always like that the last school day before a show. Friday was our last chance to work through the *Wizard* and we knew we'd need all the work we could get.

Nobody really does any schoolwork the day before the show. Not just the Drama Geeks. I mean, the entire school. All the teachers know to keep the lessons light since any number of students can be called out of class at various points in the day to work scenes, get fitted for last-minute costumes, or help finish painting the set.

Or to just skip class. But the teachers don't need to know that.

This year, I expected that it would be like a second all-day rehearsal. With Sam now obviously the lone Dorothy, there was a lot of work still to do.

"What will this day be like, I wonder?" Sam sang the opening lines of "I Have Confidence" as she came up to my locker.

What could I do? I sang back. *"What will my future be?"* Too bad I hit a really sour note on that "be." I guess I'm not destined to play the part of Maria in *The Sound of Music*.

Pity.

"How many classes do you think we can get out of today?" Sam asked, saving me from having to continue a song way out of my range.

"Considering how much work needs to be done on the show? I'd say we could probably get out of classes we don't even take."

"Too true."

I guess we were ignoring that huge white elephant in the hall; the one that was trumpeting the fact that we still had one day of Heather's machinations to contend with. Fine. If she wanted to play that game, I was totally up for it.

Unfortunately, the imaginary trumpeting I heard wasn't an elephant. It was the sound of a parade led by Headmaster Collins and consisting of Mr. Randall and Heather Mayflower.

The wicked witch of Orion was about to strike.

"Ms. Lawson," Headmaster Collins said as he approached us. "May I take a look inside your locker?"

Sam took a moment to size up the situation. Having watched many movies and TV shows with her, I knew she was well versed in drama to know that the moment someone asks to examine your locker, your room, or your intentions, that's the last thing you want to happen.

"What's wrong?" she asked, stalling.

"I need to see inside your locker," the headmaster said.

Sensing scandal, people in the hall started lingering by their own lockers to watch.

I saw Heather looking all smug beside the headmaster. Her reaction gave me a few ideas on what could be in the locker. My mind was racing with ways to distract this little ensemble as well as the crowd who was quickly gathering around us. The only thing I could come up with was yelling, "Fire!" and pulling the alarm. I doubt anyone would fall for it, but at least the sprinklers going off would clear the hallways. None of the girls—and few of the guys—would stick around to let their hair get messed.

"Is there something you're looking for?" Sam asked. She was now searching the halls. I wasn't sure what she was looking for, but I started looking too.

"Headmaster Collins," Heather said. "Sam's obviously hiding something. You should just—"

"Heather, please," Mr. Randall said.

Heather hit us all with one of the deepest sighs she had ever let out. Seriously. I nearly fell over from the force of the wind. The only person who seemed to be actually falling for it was the headmaster. Then again, *he* was the only one it was probably intended for, so the sigh was doing its job. "I turned over my purse as soon as you asked me the other day," she said.

Well, that wasn't entirely true. But I didn't think pointing that out at the moment was a good idea.

Suddenly, it was totally clear to me what she was up to. But in case anyone didn't make the connection, Heather made it for us. "Of course, I never expected to find *her mother's test* in my purse." Thank you, Heather . . . But she continued, "Maybe Sam knows there's something in her locker she doesn't want you to see."

I could practically see the debate raging in Sam's mind. There was nothing she could do. The school policy on locker searches was pretty clear. If Sam didn't open it, the headmaster would be totally free to do it himself.

Just as I was about to yell, "Fire," Sam crossed the hall to her locker. All the students in the area, including me, shifted our attention to follow her. Sam turned the combination, shot a helpless look at me over her shoulder, and opened it.

There was a collective gasp from the gathered crowd. I think they jumped the gun a bit, because nothing looked out of the ordinary from where I stood. The contents of Sam's locker included a sweater, various textbooks, two paperbacks from the Dragonriders of Pern series, her hanging crystals, and wind chimes. None of this was shocking in the least. There did look to be two items on the top of the pile, but it was hard to see what they were from where I stood.

Headmaster Collins stepped up to the locker and pulled them out for everyone to see: a CD marked CYNTHIA in block lettering and a screwdriver. Now, the gasp that came from the crowd was more appropriately timed. The CD would have been hard to explain, but there was no rule against keeping tools in your locker. If only a handful of screws hadn't dropped out of the locker when he removed the items. No doubt the screws would match up with the ones in the metal staircase in the observatory. I was amazed that Heather had enough control not to leave a taco wrapper that smelled of fish, too.

But I wasn't worried about any of that. Sam had an airtight

alibi for when Wren was attacked. All she had to do was invoke the name of Eric-the-perfect and all would be fine.

"I know this won't come as a surprise," Sam said, looking to Heather and then the headmaster. "But I don't know how that stuff got in there."

I focused my attention back on the fire alarm. All it would take was a simple pull and we could delay this discussion until a time when cooler heads could prevail.

Too bad I was frozen in place.

"Ms. Lawson," Headmaster Collins said. "What we have here is potential evidence that you caused an accident that injured another student."

Actually, what we had was some hardware. There wasn't anything that directly tied her to the crime. For that matter, the CD was just a CD at the moment. No one had even seen what was on it. But what's the point of quibbling. We all knew where this was heading.

"Can you explain what these items are doing in your locker?" he asked.

"No," Sam said.

I wanted to scream, "They were planted there by the girl smirking beside you!" but I couldn't get my mouth to work at the moment. I'm guessing Sam was having the same problem, since she was surprisingly silent as well. She was, however, still looking past the headmaster and down the hall like she was waiting for something.

I looked to Mr. Randall for help. I guess he was struck by the same silent bug that was going around. He was about to lose the one shining light in his dismal show, so I would have figured for more of a vocal reaction. Maybe a little disbelief mixed with his disappointment.

It was a shame that Hope's locker was on the whole other side of school. We could have certainly used her at the moment. Nothing ever kept her mouth shut. Her particular brand of chutzpah—see, told you I'm part Jewish—would come in handy to diffuse this situation. But for the moment, we were totally without Hope.

That was when I saw Sam's eyes light up. She found what she had been looking for. I turned in the direction of her gaze and felt a wave of relief wash over me. Hope may have been gone at the moment, but salvation was walking in our direction.

Sam's mom pushed her way through the crowd, looked at Sam, the open locker, the screwdriver and CD, and sprung into action.

"Everyone get to class," she said to the crowd. "First bell is about to ring."

Assorted moans and groans rang out around us, but Anne's glare—backed up by Headmaster Collins once he realized there was a crowd of students watching—sent most of our classmates scurrying.

Most, but not all.

Heather stuck around even though this was none of her business.

I was probably expected to leave too, but there was no way I was about to abandon my friend in her morning of need.

"Ms. Lawson," the headmaster said, addressing Anne this time. "Your daughter—"

"Do you think it's wise to have this conversation in the middle of the hallway, Headmaster Collins?" Anne asked, all sweetness and light. As concerned as the headmaster is about keeping up appearances, he is woefully unaware of how he causes scenes.

"Very well," Headmaster Collins said. "Let's adjourn to my office."

"We'll be right there," Anne said dismissively.

The headmaster clearly didn't like that, but he left, anyway. Mr. Randall followed, but Heather hung around until Anne glared at her. Finally, Heather joined the others on their way to the headmaster's office.

"Okay, Sam," Anne said. "I can pretty much figure what's going on here. Now, you know I trust you completely, but you have to be absolutely honest with me before we go into the headmaster's office. Did you have anything to do with the stuff that happened this week?"

"Anne, don't be crazy," I said, forgetting all about the rules of address while in school.

"Bryan, dear . . . please," Anne said softly. "Sam?"

"No, Mom," she said.

I was about to jump in with Sam's alibi, but Sam shot me a warning look. My first instinct was to ignore it, but I forced myself to stop. Sam may not have told her mom anything about Eric yet. If I went and blabbed about the fact they were dating, that could cross over into one of those unexpected betrayal areas.

Not that Anne would have a problem with Eric. He's one

of the best students in the school. But he *is* a student. And Sam works very hard to keep her school life and her mom's school life separate. It's doubtful that she'd want this news spread from my big mouth. So, we formed our own little three-person parade and went down to the headmaster's office, where I was told to wait outside . . . with Heather.

"I'm glad *that's* over," Heather said as the door closed behind Sam.

I went back into silent mode. The headmaster's secretary, Mrs. Bell, was not at her station, but I've often suspected she has recording devices strategically placed around the office in the event she might miss scandalous events while out for her morning coffee.

"Not that I'm surprised Sam was behind it all," Heather said. "Like I said before, she doesn't really belong here. She's not like the rest of us."

I couldn't help but wonder who this *us* was that she was referring to. I don't exactly count Heather among my inner circle.

"You don't really think Sam was sabotaging the play," I said innocently.

"Who else could it be?" Heather asked, twice as innocently. *Who else?!*

We could have one-upped each other's innocent acts all morning. Time to change track. "The thing I don't get is why she had to go all out. Couldn't she have been happy to have one whole act to herself?" I proposed.

"Some people want it all," Heather said. "And some people *deserve* it all."

"You're right," I said. "Sam does have the talent. She did deserve to be in the entire play."

"That's not what I meant."

"Oh?" I said, going back to innocent. "What *did* you mean?"

There was a brief pause while Heather took in the situation. She knew I was onto her. But she also knew there was nothing I could do about it.

"Do you really think you're going to trip me up with your oh-so-subtle questions?" Heather asked. "I've been getting around my dad's backstabbing, greedy, manipulative wives for years. And he only marries the best. So, how much do you think you're worrying me right now?"

If only my parents didn't have such a rock solid—though incredibly boring—marriage, I would be much better prepared to deal with my peer group.

"She's probably being expelled as we speak," Heather said.

"Nobody ever gets expelled from Orion," I said. The school administration works very hard to make sure it only accepts the best. In the rare cases where a student has been "transitioned out," it's only after his or her parents can arrange for an opportunity in a more challenging school environment. We tend to fail upwardly here.

"Right," Heather said. "Because whenever anyone gets close to that kind of trouble, their parents rush in and buy a building or something. What do you think Ms. Lawson can afford? Maybe a stack of outdated encyclopedias for the Klayton Library?"

I stared at her. My mouth was open, yet nothing was coming out. This was the second time today I was at a loss for something to say. And I'm usually such a chatty person.

"You look extremely happy," I finally managed.

"Why wouldn't I be?" Heather said. "I'm going to be cleared of the cheating scandal and now I get to be the one lone Dorothy. All in all, it's been a good day, and I haven't even been to one class yet."

It was killing me enough that she was being so smug about Sam's problem, but there was something else, too. Something more than our little play was behind her joyous expression.

"Oh, and did you hear about Holly?" she asked.

I couldn't imagine what her sister had to do with anything. She was still in New York basking in her burgeoning TV career, as far as I knew.

"You know how her show was picked up for next season?"

I didn't bother to respond. She knew full well that I knew, since she was the one who had told me about it the day before.

"Well," she said. "I guess the network wanted to go a different direction with her character. So, even though the show will be on this fall, she won't. Her role is being recast. It will be in all the trades on Monday. Isn't that horrible?" The bright, beaming smile on her face stood in stark contrast to what she was saying.

Still grinning about her sister's embarrassing and horrible news, Heather spun in her name-brand, ridiculously expensive shoes and bounced down the hall toward the auditorium. I swear I could hear her maniacal cackle echoing through the halls of the building.

Or that could have been my imagination.

Either way, in case you weren't paying attention earlier, please allow me to reiterate: Heather is eeeeeevil.

Ann(i)e Get Your Gun

I stared at the door to the headmaster's office, focusing my mental abilities in the hope that I could see what was going on behind his closed door. Or at the very least, try to hear what everyone inside was saying.

Maybe I shouldn't have been listening so intently because when Hope came into the outer office yelling, "What the heck is going on?!" she came pretty close to giving me a heart attack.

Once the pitter-patter of my heart returned to normal, I quickly filled her in on the situation, highlighting the Eric involvement in the story and my feelings about all that. I gave her a moment to absorb what I told her, figuring she would come up with the perfect plan to convince Sam that she had to play the Eric card.

Imagine how disappointed I was when Hope said, "Yeah, I get that. I don't know that I'd want to get my new boyfriend in trouble either. It's not a good way to start a relationship."

Considering this *relationship* consisted of one date and a make-out session somewhere on campus, I didn't necessarily agree . . . and proceeded to tell Hope as much . . . with expletives, even. I'm guessing the headmaster's door was steel reinforced because he didn't open it to wash my mouth out with soap. No wonder I couldn't hear anything earlier.

"You done?" Hope finally asked.

"For now," I said.

"Good. I know firsthand how hard it is to get someone out of a practice. Especially right before the final game. If Drew had done something like that for me, I don't know that I'd be all quick to turn him in."

"Really?" I asked, thinking about her always shaky relationship. "You wouldn't? Even if you could be expelled?"

"Okay, bad example," Hope said. "But, still, I understand Sam's situation."

"Yeah, but . . ." I didn't have a chance to figure out what I was going to say next because the door to Headmaster Collins's office finally opened. Mr. Randall, Anne, and Sam walked out, each looking more stunned than the next. It was all we could do not to pounce on them.

My heart broke a little when Sam couldn't even look at me or Hope.

"Why don't you go home, honey," Anne said softly. "I can get a ride home after school."

Sam simply nodded and walked out of the room. She didn't even bother to say good-bye. We watched her perp-walk down the hall like she had just been tried and convicted.

Once I was sure Sam was out of earshot, I turned and strained not to shout, "She was expelled?!"

"Oh," Mrs. Bell said as she came in from the other direction holding a steaming cup of coffee. "Did I miss something?"

"No, Mrs. Bell. Nothing at all," Anne said as she and Mr. Randall ushered us out of the office.

"Sam hasn't been expelled," Anne said once we were in the empty hall. "There wasn't enough evidence to prove she actually pulled the prank on Wren or put Cindy's pictures up online. Headmaster Collins wants to let things settle for the weekend, then he'll launch a full investigation next week."

"He's calling the attack on Wren a prank?" I asked.

Anne shrugged. "There's no way to prove it was done intentionally to hurt her."

"In the meantime," Mr. Randall added, "Sam is out of the show." He seemed even more upset about that than we were. If that's even possible.

"But that's not fair," I said.

"You know how easy it is to break into lockers around here," Hope added. "Anyone could have planted that stuff."

"*Heather* could have planted that stuff," I insisted.

"Believe me," Anne said. "I already reminded the headmaster about that. The locker part, not Heather. We can't go throwing around false accusations. Unless you two know anything for sure?"

There was one thing I *did* know for sure. I was about to tell Anne about Sam's alibi when I felt the crushing stomp of

Hope's steel-toe boot on my Chucks. (Of all days to opt for the canvas sneakers instead of my hard leather Skechers.)

Even though I didn't say anything, Anne must have seen something in my expression. Pain, mostly. "Do you know something, Bryan?" she asked.

I didn't need to look at Hope to know the expression on her face. "Not really," I said as my toes throbbed.

"If you'll excuse me," Mr. Randall said. "I have to find Heather and start working act one with her."

"She's in the auditorium waiting for you," I said.

"Of course she is," he said as he turned and went down the hall.

"How serious is this?" Hope asked. "Can Sam really be expelled?"

"I can get my parents involved," I said, knowing full well that my mom lived for this kind of fight. And she *loves* Sam to boot. "Heather seemed to think that . . . well, she kind of said . . ."

"Yes," Anne said, "I can imagine what Heather said. And thanks for the offer, but Sam's got more on her side than you might think."

I wasn't sure what Anne was talking about at first, but she quickly cleared up my confusion. Turns out, Sam has something even better than money. She has publicity.

Like I wrote earlier, Sam is the only student here on the teacher-discount plan. She may not have a building named after her grandparents, but that doesn't mean she can't be useful to the school in other ways. Apparently, she is a great press release for equal opportunity education.

Any time anyone went after the school for being elitist, Headmaster Collins would trot Sam out as an example—the *only* example—of how the school benefits the less financially endowed. It is, quite possibly, the most patronizingly offensive thing I have ever heard in my life. And yet, it's also a great bargaining chip. Because how bad would the press be if Orion Academy's one true charity case—Anne's words, not mine—was expelled without a thorough investigation and actual proof that Sam was behind the attacks?

But that didn't get Sam back in the show.

Considering the stolen test had come from Anne's class, Headmaster Collins felt that clue pointed to Sam's guilt as well. As such, he reinstated Heather as a Dorothy. Correction: The lone Dorothy.

I was wondering if it was too late to return the show tickets. There was no way I wanted my mom to have to sit through the travesty that awaited us all.

"I should get to class," Anne said. "No telling what the sophomores have done to my room by now. You should get to class too. Do you want me to write you a note?"

"No, we'll get excused for rehearsal," Hope said. "That's where Mr. Clark probably thinks we are, anyway."

When Anne said good-bye I could hear the concern in her voice. I still wanted to tell her about Sam's out, but my toes couldn't take another assault. That didn't mean I had given up the fight.

"Is there some reason we couldn't tell Anne about Eric?" I asked as Hope and I moved toward Hall Hall.

"Because it's not our place to say."

"Forgive me if I don't think Sam is in her right mind at the moment. She could be expelled."

"Do you really think she'll let it go that far?" Hope asked. "It's not the end of the world yet."

"It's the end of the show," I said.

"Please," Hope said. "This show was over before the first rehearsal."

"There's that old 'show must go on' spirit," I said. "Mr. Randall would be so proud."

"Like he's not thinking the same thing," Hope said. To emphasize her point, she opened the auditorium door. We were greeted by the shrill sound of Heather's singing.

"If you ask me, Sam's the lucky one," Hope said.

"You have an odd outlook on life."

"Just promise me you won't go making things worse," Hope said.

For the second time in as many days I made a promise I had no intention of keeping. It bothered me more to lie to Hope than it did to Heather, but only a little bit.

Sleuth

By lunch I was beginning to suspect that Hope was coming around to my side. Certainly her attitude was darkening over the whole situation as the day progressed.

"A half dozen people have come up to me already, blaming Sam for ruining the play," she said as she sat at the Drama Geeks' table.

Today we were joined by the regulars, Tasha—who was paging through a book of Edward Gorey's morbid artwork—and Jimmy—who was busy highlighting his prompt book with the music and light cues for the show. Luckily, Wren's boyfriend, Jason, was also there, and he was surprisingly quick to jump to Sam's defense.

"That's ridiculous," he said. "You tell Sam that Wren doesn't think that at all. There's no way Sam would hurt anyone. Not to mention that she doesn't need to. This play should be the least of her concerns. She's so much better than that."

"How is Wren?" I asked.

"Milking it," he replied. Not exactly the doting boyfriend, is he? "It's just a sprain. She could do the play. But since she can't shine as the prima jitterbugger, she doesn't want to do it at all."

"Does she have any idea who *did* do it?" Hope asked.

"No," Jason said, trading his exasperation for real concern. "Once the lights went out, she couldn't see anything." I noticed his hand was squeezing his Snapple bottle in anger. Maybe this relationship would last beyond Wren's graduation. "I don't understand why she would go into the observatory alone after everything that's happened this week."

That was the question of the day for most people. Not me, though. My burning question was, "Who was the saboteur?" The answer was pretty obvious:

Jax.

Heather's boyfriend had the motive. Namely, Heather. He had the means. It wasn't too hard to loosen a few screws. But I kept getting stuck on the opportunity. If it was such a big deal that Eric bailed on soccer practice, the same could be said for Jax. If he did miss practice, wasn't that a way to move his name to the top of the suspect list?

Jax could be the proof that I was looking for. And, unlike his Machiavellian girlfriend, I knew I could trick him into admitting the truth. There was only one problem with my plan.

"What is Heather doing here?" I asked. Because as soon as

I looked over to where Jax was sitting, her blond hair was the first thing I saw.

"She's *here?*" Hope's head swung around in the direction I was looking.

"Nice to know she can take time out of rehearsal to grab a bite with her boyfriend," Jason added. I think my fellow Scarecrow took this play more seriously than anyone in the school. Actually, he generally takes performing more seriously than anyone in the school (with the possible exception of Sam—in spite of her current attitude).

Heather's lunch break made perfect sense to me. Aside from the fact that Heather didn't think she needed all that much work, she probably also didn't want to leave Jax alone at lunch. Especially knowing that I was on the case.

It's possible that she wasn't worried about me specifically, but it was a big risk leaving him unsupervised during the sociable part of the day. Heather had too much riding on tomorrow's show for her plan to fall apart at the last minute.

But I didn't need to force an admission out of Jax to redirect suspicion in Heather's direction. I only needed to prove that he wasn't at practice. Luckily, I had one of the few breaks of the week happen. Coach Zach was on lunch duty.

In light of what happened on Monday, all the teachers had been reporting to duty on time for once. This would eventually start to drop off as we got further away from Suze's accident, but for now I was going to use it to my benefit.

I was about to get up from the table when I heard the opening notes of the song "Defying Gravity" from *Wicked* emerging from Hope's bag. "That's me," she said as she pulled out her cell phone.

"You get reception here?" I asked. *Nobody* gets reception at school. I had to find out what plan she was on.

Hope checked to make sure Coach Zach didn't see her answering her phone. She looked at the caller ID and answered the phone with an unusually cheery voice. "Hi! Did you get it? . . . I told you . . . I know . . . I can do that. . . . That's great! But, I better go before someone sees me on the phone. . . . Love you, too. Bye!"

She closed the phone, dropped it back in her bag, and resumed eating.

"Care to tell me what that was about?" I asked.

"Nope."

I waited for something more, but she just kept eating. I suspected that the call had something to do with Suze's stolen sketchbook, but Hope was still keeping mum on that. I decided to deal with one mystery at a time.

"Be right back," I said as I went to speak with Coach Zach. I knew that I couldn't just come out and ask him if Jax was at practice. That would be too obvious. Coach Zach might try to protect one of his players. No, I had to be crafty about this. And not in the way Suze is crafty. I meant manipulative. I had to be Heather.

Talk about an acting challenge.

"Hey, Coach Zach," I said.

"Hey, Bry," he replied, ignoring my cringe. I hate when people call me "Bry." "Let me guess. You've decided to give up on your dream of acting and come out for the team?"

"Obviously you've forgotten about that baseball game in gym last month," I said.

"I've tried," Coach Zach said as he bent to rub his shin. "But I keep getting a reminder when it rains."

Note to all aspiring players: When swinging the bat, maintain a firm grip. Do not let it slip from your hands. Do not let it fly across the baseball field. And, most of all, do *not* let it hit the person who determines your grade for the class.

Changing subject.

"But I am interested in soccer," I said, hoping that if I got him talking about his team, he might let something slip. "For an article in *The Star*." The odds were pretty good that he didn't know I am just a photographer for the paper, not one of the writers. "About the work it takes to be a soccer player. Like how you run your practices. Take yesterday, for example."

"We didn't have a full practice yesterday," he said. "I had the guys do a cross-country run. Soccer players have to be runners, too, you know."

"You don't happen to run with them, do you?"

Coach Zach laughed.

Yeah, I thought not. So he'd have no idea if Jax took a detour during the run. No one on the team probably would have noticed either. And no one would be able to prove that he had gone to the observatory for the attack.

Hmph. That got me nowhere.

The Wiz

Throughout the rest of the day I tried getting in touch with Sam by calling, e-mailing, and IMing. I even considered carrier pigeon, but where would I get one on such short notice? If only Orion Academy had an owlery.

It didn't matter. Sam would not pick up, reply, or respond. I could only imagine what she would have done to the poor pigeon that showed up at her window.

Driving Electra over to Sam's apartment was an option, but not really a good one. If she wasn't answering the phone, she wouldn't know I was outside the security gate wanting to be buzzed in. It was silly to drive all the way to Santa Monica to do my impression of Stanley Kowalski from *A Streetcar Named Desire*, yelling, "Sam!" from the pavement instead of "Stella!"

I wondered where I could print up some "Free Sam" T-shirts. That seemed to be the only plausible course of action at that point.

I wasn't the only one in a quandary. Mr. Randall had spent the rest of the day—minus lunch—working with Heather one on one. He didn't even bother to involve the rest of the cast. His thought process was that we all knew our parts well enough and we could work around Heather.

Work around the lead of the show, you ask?

Yeah, it was pretty clear to all involved that Mr. Randall had simply given up.

Everyone had lost that "show must go on" spirit.

That's why instead of going over one last polish of the show with my friends after school, I was once again sitting in my stainless-steel kitchen eating a Pop-Tart. This time it was Brown Sugar and Cinnamon, for those of you keeping track at home.

I sat, staring at my Pop-Tart, thinking about the events of the past week. I guess things really did all start with that falling lamp. An accident. It had to be. Even Heather wasn't good enough to simulate metal fatigue. But maybe it inspired her; gave her the idea that she could be the lone Dorothy if other "accidents" happened along the way. From that point, everything else had been her doing.

It really was brilliant, now that I thought of it. Jax had spilled his drink on Sam Monday, sending her out of the pavilion and, more importantly, away from our table. Even though we all knew she was changing shirts, someone else might think it was an opportunity to switch Suze's taco while she was supposed to be out of the room. We were all focused on Hope's dress at the time, so nobody would have noticed.

And that's why nobody noticed Heather doing that very thing.

Tuesday was pure brilliance. Anyone could have had access to Cynthia's locker. Sam wouldn't have even needed to know that the locker was so easy to break into. *Most* of the lockers in school are that way. The mere fact that not every piece of evidence pointed directly to Sam made her look better at covering her tracks. Until the CD turned up in Sam's locker, that is.

Wednesday, Heather took herself off the suspect list by making herself a victim. Notice how she used Sam's own mom to trap her? Out of all the tests she could have stolen, it wasn't merely a coincidence that she had taken the English final.

And we all know what she did to Wren—and me—yesterday. Which brings me to Friday afternoon in my kitchen, still staring at my Pop-Tart.

That left two questions. One: How did Heather know Sam wasn't going to have a usable alibi? And two: How did Jax get the coach to schedule a run to the beach instead of regular practice? Were these things just luck?

Oh, and three: How could I get the answers to these questions before the show opened?

And, of course, one more: Why wouldn't Sam give up Eric as her alibi? Isn't the school show just as important as some soccer game? Aren't her needs as important as Eric's? Aren't hers even more important since she's never going to get a college scholarship with this kind of thing on her record?

Okay, so that was a lot more than two questions. But it was the end of the list that was the most upsetting.

Why *was* Sam not telling anyone where she was yesterday? Honestly, I find it hard to believe that Coach Zach would bench his star player from the finals just for missing one practice. Oh, sure, Eric would have to be punished with some kind of detention, but not in a way that would risk the end of a winning season.

I couldn't help wondering why Sam refused to tell me what was really going on. Or why she was totally ignoring me all day. I had nothing to do with any of this. Well, except for the fact that I was a constant reminder that she had a way out. All she had to do was betray the guy she only recently started seeing.

It finally happened. A guy had come between us. And not in the way I had ever feared.

I dropped my Pop-Tart on my plate. My appetite was gone.

"Hey, Little Prince," a sugary sweet voice with a hint of a giggle said as the kitchen door swung open.

"Hi, Mom," I replied as the woman of the house came breezing into the room carrying a box full of doggie duds. She dropped them on the kitchen table and blew by me so quickly that I knew she wasn't alone. She pulled a doggie gate out of the pantry and locked it into the doorway leading into her pristine museum home.

"All clear," she yelled out.

I turned toward the kitchen door as one of my oldest and dearest friends came barreling in. "Hey, Mal!" I said as a seventy-five-pound black Lab came bounding into the kitchen and jumped up on me. "Who's my favorite girl?" I asked in that kind of baby talk we all instinctively revert to whenever we're around adorable animals.

Mal—which is short for Maleficent—is the closest thing to a cousin that I have. Since both my parents are only children, my family circle includes my parents' closest friends. And no friend is closer to my mom than her bestest friend and business partner, Blaine.

"Hey, kiddo," Blaine said as he came in behind Mal carrying two more boxes of my mom's creations. Mom is the artist behind the business. Blaine is the brains. Even with the bulk in his arms, he managed to free a hand to muss my hair. Leave it to Blaine to catch me without my fedora on.

Just so we're clear, Blaine is the only person in this—or any other—world permitted to muss my hair. Or to call me "kiddo."

I know what you're thinking, by the way. Because his name is Blaine and he's co-owner of a boutique that designs clothing for the prissy, pampered pets of the prissy, pampered Hollywood elite, you've probably gotten this picture in your head. Let me guess: a stunningly tanned, perfectly coiffed, gay man with a lisp, wearing neatly ironed clothes in hues of pink and white?

Wrong.

Blaine is a 250-pound, bald black man who could snap you in two like a twig. But he *is* gay. In fact, he plays rugby on the only straight-friendly rugby team in L.A.

And now you're probably wondering why—if my mom's best friend in the entire world is a totally well-adjusted and perfectly happy gay man—why then, oh why, am I so reluctant to come out of my own closet?

Good question.

"Bryan. Table," Mom said. She likes to keep the sentences simple when I'm in trouble. I took it to mean that she didn't like the fact I had dropped bits of Pop-Tart on the center island.

I quickly wiped up the crumbs. "What? It's *stainless*."

"Such sass," Blaine said, chucking me lightly on the arm. I say lightly because if he really wanted to hit me, he'd knock me off the stool. "Don't you talk to your mother that way."

Blaine was smiling as he said this because we both knew the response it would get.

First there was the look of wide-eyed horror. Then, the sharp intake of breath. Followed by, "Oh, you know I was just messin'. Eat away!"

Mom prefers to think of herself as a best friend instead of a *mom*. At times, the friend status clashes with her more natural instincts as a neat freak.

"Thanks, Mom," I said, taking a big bite out of my Pop-Tart, not caring where the crumbs landed. Mom can be pretty cool when she wants to be. At least she doesn't make me call her by her first name like so many parents around Malibu force their children to do. It's one thing for me to call Sam's mom by her given name. That's okay, because I think of her as a friend, and *Sam* still calls her "Mom." It's another thing entirely when your own parent expects you to be so informal with them.

"Give me a second," Mom said to Blaine as she climbed over the doggie gate, "and I'll get that thing I promised you."

"The magazine article on the new pet hotels," Blaine reminded her.

"I know," Mom said as she left the kitchen. Part of the reason Mom keeps the house so clean is because it's the only way she can keep track of anything. She's definitely where my artistic side comes from. Luckily, it doesn't also come with her lack of organizational skills.

I gave Mal a good squeeze as she tried to climb up on my lap. Even though there was no room for the two of us on the stool, I didn't mind. She was exactly what I needed. We can't have pets of our own because of my dad's allergies. Not that he has anything near the level of Suze's. I think he's just not a big fan of animals. Which is why when I'm down I usually have to go to Mal. Thankfully, someone knew I needed her today.

"Spill," Blaine said.

I looked back at the counter. "I didn't spill anything. It's all clean."

"Very funny," he said, pulling up a stool. "Now, do you want to tell me what's bothering you?"

Did I mention that Blaine is like scary psychic when it comes to me? He always knows when something's up. Or when I've done something wrong. I think it has something to do with the world maintaining balance. In light of an often absent father and a sweet, but oblivious mom, the powers-that-be have put a person in my life who doesn't let me get away with anything. Ever.

Sometimes, it can be a real pain in the ass.

This? Was not one of those times.

I quickly found myself spilling out the details of the entire week, from the falling lamp, to the aborted prom date, to Sam not talking to me. I doubt most of it made any sense, but Blaine listened quietly, only interrupting for a few clarifications.

Once I finally finished babbling, Blaine sat quietly for a moment. I suspected that he was about to come up with some of his traditional words of wisdom. I waited in silence until he finally spoke.

"Stop being an idiot," he said.

This was no surprise, as his advice often opens up by indicating I had missed the obvious.

"First thing, first," he continued expanding on my alleged idiocy. "You need to get Sam back in the show."

"But she won't—"

He held up a hand that immediately silenced me.

"In my many years of being friends with your mother, I have learned numerous valuable lessons." This was going to be good. "One of the most valuable is when I cannot get what I want *from* her, I often find it helps to go *around* her."

Which is how I found myself sitting on the front steps of Eric Whitman's house the very next day.

Old Times

It was another typically sunny Malibu afternoon. The morning haze had burned off, leaving nothing but a totally blue sky over my head. But that didn't lighten my mood any. Nor did it darken my complexion, sad to say.

Mr. Whitman's housekeeper had told me over the phone when he'd be back. I had expected to get Eric's dad, but I guess he went with Eric and Drew to New Mexico. I was still having trouble thinking of Drew playing college soccer. He's okay enough, but it never really struck me that it was anything more than a pastime. He has been playing soccer for years, but never with the kind of intensity Eric showed on the field.

I had a lot of time to think about this since their plane was apparently late. Either that or they stopped for lunch on the way home.

Eric lives in one of the really, *really* expensive homes down by the water, with the beach as his backyard. For decades the residents on his street had been in battle with the county over that particular stretch of beach. Technically, it was supposed to be a public beach, but considering the neighborhood was built with about a half-foot of space between the houses, it wasn't really conducive to tourist traffic.

Eventually the county won out and opened up a couple throughways for people to get from the street to the sand. Now, on any given day you can see various people tramping across the private driveways looking for beach access.

From time to time, people in unfortunate swimwear would stop by Electra, tap on her door frame, and ask me for directions. But mostly, they just yelled out to one another, "I think we go down this way!" This was usually followed by the sound of an angry dog barking because the tourists had guessed wrong and found themselves on private property.

I spent the rest of the time enjoying the ocean breeze while safely sitting in the shade of Electra and reading the late, great Katharine Hepburn's memoir. The book was a little self-indulgent for my tastes, but, ignoring some of her more outrageous flights of fancy, you have to admit that woman was a heck of a dame.

Two hours after I had estimated they would be home, the Whitmans' tricked-out black SUV finally backed into the short driveway. I could see the surprise on Eric's face through the lightly tinted windshield as I got out of Electra. I assumed the shadow in the backseat was Drew.

"Bryan Stark!" Mr. Whitman said as he stepped down from his oversize vehicle. His perfect smile and even more perfectly sculpted hair were both shining in the sunlight. "What a pleasant surprise."

"Hello, Mr. Whitman," I said as I reached him. My hand disappeared into his as we shook. Mr. Whitman always has this larger-than-life personality that could eclipse anyone in the room. Eric clearly takes after his dad, while his little brother, Matthew, is the introvert in the family. I guess Matthew was at a friend's for the weekend, because he wasn't around at the time.

"Come inside, come inside," Mr. Whitman said, ushering me indoors.

The looks of surprise had not left Eric's or Drew's face as they followed us through the foyer into the expansive living room accented by dark wood and forest green wallpaper. *This* was a room of men. The darkness looked totally out of place against the beach backdrop, but the décor was more of a statement than a lifestyle. The place was very different before Eric's mom ran off with the tennis instructor from their country club a few years ago.

The only thing that saved Mrs. Whitman's exit from being a total cliché was that the tennis instructor was a rather attractive woman named Claire. Eric traditionally spends the holidays and one month out of the summer with them in the Hamptons.

"Have a seat. Have a seat," Mr. Whitman said as he deposited me on the brown suede couch. The man did have a penchant for repeating himself.

"Come in, boys," he said to his son and Drew, who were still standing in the doorway. "Come in."

Eric and Drew looked at each other. There was a definite chill in the room, and I have to admit it was emanating from me. They could tell I was in the mood for a showdown of some kind. Understandably, they didn't have a clue what it was about.

They eventually did as Mr. Whitman instructed, sitting on the two leather chairs at the entrance of the room.

"Look at this," Mr. Whitman said as he held his arms out toward us. "The Three Musketeers, together again."

Hold on! Let me clarify that comment.

There were never any *Three* Musketeers. Eric and I have never been friends, much less as close as Musketeers. Or Mouseketeers, even.

But, Drew . . . that's another story entirely.

A long time ago, we used to be friends. *More* than friends, actually. We were *best* friends. Inseparable since kindergarten. The originators of the Vampire Pact. Except back then it was the Super Secret Agent Pact. We agreed that if one of us was ever recruited by a Top Secret Ultra Black Ops Government Agency, he would insist that the other was also brought in. That way we could be partners in saving the world from foreign powers.

We were the *Two* Musketeers. But somewhere along the way— soccer camp the summer before sixth grade, to be specific—Eric came into the picture and started following us around. Insert image of little puppy dog here, if it so pleases you.

But the status quo hadn't totally changed. For years, it was Drew and me with Eric tagging along. Until one day . . . it wasn't anymore.

It was taking a while for Mr. Whitman to catch on to the new dynamic, so we all had to sit through a round of questions about my family, my schoolwork, and assorted personal details that I'm sure Mr. Whitman would forget the moment I left. That took up a good five minutes before we were both searching for something to talk about.

"It looks like you men have things to discuss," Mr. Whitman finally said. I suspect he caught on to the fact that he and I were the only ones who had spoken since we all entered the house. "I'll be in my study. Bryan, it was good to see you. Good to see you, indeed."

"You too, Mr. Whitman," I mumbled.

As soon as Mr. Whitman left, the room fell into silence. Eric and Drew were waiting for me to say something, but I wasn't even sure where to begin.

"How was the trip?" I asked.

"Fine," they said in unison.

"Are you really thinking of going to New Mexico?" I asked Drew. "I thought you always wanted to go somewhere on the East Coast."

"I'm looking at different places," Drew said. "I don't know what I want. I've got a while to figure it out."

"I get that," I said. I had no clue where I wanted to go either.

I guess Eric wasn't into small talk, because he jumped in with, "Is something wrong?"

"Why would you think that?" I asked, switching to full on attitude. "Just because I visit on a Saturday afternoon? Obviously something must be wrong? I couldn't just stop by to say hi?"

Honestly, I had no idea what I was saying.

"I'm sorry," Eric said, matching my attitude. "Have I *done* something to you?"

"Oh, *that's* precious," I said. "Like you—"

"Hey!" Drew interrupted. "Knock it off!"

That managed to shut Eric and me up. But we still sat seething at each other. This kind of thing has been happening between Eric and me for years. I guess, technically, I'm the one responsible for the attitude. But, can you *really* blame me this time? How many of my best friends does he want to take from me?

"Bryan," Drew said, calmly. "What brings you here?"

"Sam," I said.

"Is she okay?" Eric quickly asked.

"No," I said, reluctantly giving him points for being concerned. I quickly took them away too. "No thanks to you."

"What did I do?" he asked.

"Well, first of all, you couldn't keep your hands to yourself."

"Hey, Sam never said you two were together."

"What are you talking about?!" I can't believe he thought I was jealous.

"What are *you* talking about?" Though I guess I could understand why he might be confused.

Realizing that we were getting nowhere, I stopped the attack and quickly brought Eric and Drew up to speed on everything they'd missed since leaving for New Mexico on Thursday. "And she's doing it for you," I added at the end, driving home the point that I blamed Eric for Sam's situation. "She's giving up her role in the show so you don't lose your place on the team."

I let that last comment hang in the air for a moment. Eric didn't even bother defending himself. He just sat there. Silently. You'd think he would at least say something. But no.

Eventually, he got up off his chair and went to the phone.

"What are you doing?" I asked.

He simply pushed a button and waited. Not even bothering to look at me.

"Headmaster Collins?" Eric said into the phone. "This is Eric Whitman."

Did I mention that most of the school parents have the headmaster's private residence on speed dial?

I sat back on the couch, trying not to look at Drew, while Eric explained to the headmaster why Sam couldn't have possibly attacked Wren on Thursday. Eric even went so far as to take full responsibility for his actions for cutting soccer practice and admitted that he was prepared for whatever punishment the coach felt necessary.

He did it all of his own free will and without any prompting from me.

Lest you think that selfless act of nobility changed my mind about him. Sorry. Wrong. He's still a total asshat as far as I'm concerned.

Well, maybe not *total*.

The Mousetrap

Jimmy handed me a program and I immediately opened it to check my name. It was spelled right, for a change. More often than not, the printer "corrects" the spelling to "Brian," ignoring the fact that "Bryan" is a perfectly acceptable form of the word. Personally, I think "Brian Stark" looks like a third-rate agent specializing in dog acts or people who used to guest-star on *Star Trek*. At least *"Bryan* Stark" has some flare to it.

Or not.

I carefully slipped the program into my script so I could add it to the Bryan stack when I got home. If I was right, the Bryans had finally caught up to the Brians. I then stuck the script in my back pocket because I knew I'd be checking it at least a hundred times before I set foot onstage. I get a little crazy about my lines on show nights.

Still, there's nothing like the excitement of being backstage on opening night. Or on closing night. You can probably imagine how frenetic things are when your opening night *is* closing night. One night to get the show right. To hit your marks. To know your lines. No chance to fix the mistakes or try something new.

One night to succeed or fail.

Then, throw in double, triple, and quadruple casting, add a wild week of losing every one of your leads to the general chaos, and you might start to understand what the Roberta Kittridge Dressing Room looked like with only fifteen minutes to curtain.

Thankfully, we have a fairly large dressing room. The space is divided by a row of folding screens to separate the boys from the girls. The segregating of boys and girls is more of a *suggestion* than a reality. With a cast of dozens getting into costumes and makeup, there really isn't enough space for modesty in the dressing room.

"You've all got your programs. Are you happy?" Jimmy said as he shifted from passive-obsessive to obsessive-aggressive. Show nights always did this to him. "This is your fifteen-minute call. I'll be back for your ten-minute call in five minutes."

"You mean four minutes and fifty-nine seconds," I said, hoping to lighten his mood.

"Four minutes and fifty-eight seconds," Sam added from beside me.

Jimmy glared at us, yelled, "Actors!" and left the room in a huff.

Now, just because Sam was sitting next to me and we were riffing off each other, do not think that all was forgiven. She hadn't managed to speak directly *to* me since she arrived forty-five minutes earlier.

With Eric's confession, it was finally clear that someone had stuck the hardware in Sam's locker hoping to frame her. From there, the headmaster took the logical leap that the copy of the CD with naked photos of Cindy had also been planted. With no real evidence, he was forced to reinstate Sam in the show.

At the same time, there was still no evidence that indicated Heather was the one behind the frame-up. So she stayed as the act two Dorothy while Sam came back in for act one.

The show was now set to open with flair, but end in tragedy.

The jury was still out on what Eric's punishment would be for skipping practice. I could only assume that was the reason Sam still wasn't speaking to me. That made it all the more difficult for us to get ready, since Jimmy had assigned us seats next to each other. And the first rule of show night is do not mess with Jimmy's organizational system.

"Promise you won't laugh!" Hope yelled from the boys' side of the dressing screen. Sam and I were sitting at the long table on the girls' side, already in costume, trying not to look at each other. She was in makeup, but I didn't have to put mine on until intermission.

Without acknowledging each other, Sam and I were already snickering in anticipation. "Promise!" we yelled back simultaneously. What was one more broken promise this week, anyway?

"You're already laughing!" Hope yelled back.

At this, we cracked up. You'd think this shared laugh before the show would bring us together. I thought it would. But when I looked over to Sam, she was looking pointedly in the opposite direction.

Hope is not one to embarrass easily. We could only imagine what she looked like since she refused to let us see her in costume until this moment. Hence the laughter.

"Get out here," Sam yelled.

"Fine."

Hope stepped out from behind the dressing screen.

We both sat stone-faced, willing ourselves not to laugh.

I can't speak for Sam, but it was some of the best acting I have ever done.

As Glinda the Good Witch, Hope was a vision in fluffy pink taffeta on top of more crinoline than in an entire production of *Grease*. She looked not unlike a giant pile of cotton candy. I don't think I'd ever seen her in so much color. And the whole black outfit Goth-Ick look only started when we got to high school.

"Oh, shut up," Hope said, even though we were both sitting in stony silence.

"I think you look . . . *beautiful*," I said, stretching out that last word into way more syllables than nature had intended.

"How did Mr. Randall get you into an outfit that can be found on the color wheel?" Sam asked.

"Oh, I made my little adjustments," Hope said conspiratorially. "I'm wearing a black bra underneath."

"We can see," I said.

"Pink taffeta isn't as concealing as one might think," Sam added.

Hope's eyes bugged out and she ran back to the guys' side. I assume she went behind the privacy curtain for a quick underwear change.

"You didn't see the bra either, did you?" I asked.

Sam smiled at me slyly.

Even when we weren't speaking, we were totally in sync.

I figured this was my opening. "Look—"

"After the show," she said. So much for being in sync. "I need to get into character."

I guess I couldn't blame her. Thirteen minutes and twenty-five seconds to curtain wasn't the best time to have an emotional discussion. As she finished up her makeup, Jason saddled up to our area.

"Break a leg, guys," he said.

"Break a leg," we replied.

Even though I knew this had been Jason's preshow ritual for years, it seemed a little inappropriate for him to be wishing everyone in the cast to break a leg. Considering what had happened to Wren the other day and all.

"Hey, Bryan," he continued. "I just took a peek through the curtain. There's a strange guy sitting with your mom."

"Thanks, Jason," I said as he moved on to wish broken legs to the rest of the cast.

The "strange guy" Jason was joking about was obviously my dad. It was nice of Jason to let me know Dad had made it in time. Not that this was a surprise. No matter where in the world Dad is, he always makes it to a show before the curtain goes up. Since his mysterious business travel began back when I was around nine, he has never missed one performance, one birthday, one holiday, or any other special event. He is great on the big stuff. It's the day-to-day he needs to work on.

Sam was going through her preshow vocal exercises when I heard her stop halfway through. Something must have been wrong, because she never stops in the middle of her exercises. It's a ritual. When I turned toward her, I saw her looking for something.

"Where's Toto?" she asked. It was more of a rhetorical question. She wasn't speaking to me directly, but I took it as an opening.

"Where did you see him last?" I asked.

"Right here." She pointed to the end of the table. "I was working with him before Hope showed us her outfit."

"No worries," I said. "Just go to the prop closet and get one of the spares."

She let out an annoyed huff and went over to the closet. I know she was upset because she had been working with that specific Toto all week, but a stuffed dog is a stuffed dog. Any dog will do.

"The Totos are gone," Sam said. "All of them."

I did a quick scan of the dressing room. The place was packed with people buzzing all over. Anyone could have easily moved the Totos. Accidents happen, especially on opening night. But I knew this was no accident. This was . . .

"Heather," we said in unison.

We looked over at the other Dorothy's station, but Heather wasn't there. We were about to tear apart the dressing room when Sam noticed Heather walking out the door. She had a Toto under her arm.

"That's it," Sam said as she stormed toward the door. "I've had enough."

I hurried after her, grabbing her arm. "Wait. She wants you to follow her."

"I can't go onstage without Toto."

I doubted that anyone would make that big a deal if she pantomimed the dog, but Sam is more serious about these things than I am. I knew we should have told Jimmy and let him handle it. He was back in the dressing room, but he was also clearly in panic mode. I didn't want to be responsible for sending him over the edge.

"I'll go," I said. "You stay here."

"But—"

"Just stay here," I said. I ran back to the makeup table and grabbed my camera. Just in case. Maybe I'd get a nice action shot of Heather up to no good. We could run them in this month's issue of the *Star* along with the pics of the fallen lamp.

We weren't supposed to leave the dressing room once we signed in, but I felt pretty justified in breaking the rules. I was on a mission to save the show. Still, I didn't want to incur the stage manager's wrath, no matter how noble my intentions. After making sure that Jimmy was occupied tormenting the munchkins, I hurried out of the dressing room, but the hall was already empty. I had no idea which way Heather went.

Since the gate was down to block off the rest of the school, there were only two options. Going to the right would take me out to the lobby. As most of the cast had already snuck a peek out the curtain, I knew the theater was almost entirely full at this point. It was possible that Heather was hurrying around the front to save seats for her family. *Because she's that thoughtful and considerate.*

I turned left and headed for the pavilion.

It's always weird being at school when it's closed. Since no one is supposed to be walking around, all the lights are off except for the ones at the entrance to Hall Hall. Passing by the rows of defective lockers totally alone in the dark reminded me of way too many horror movies for it not to be a little unnerving. I was so busy hearing imaginary noises all around me that I nearly missed the two voices—straining to stay at an agitated whisper—up ahead of me.

I walked even more carefully, not wanting to give away my presence. It sounded like Heather was arguing with someone. Definitely a male someone. Probably Jax.

While normally a lovers' quarrel would only be interesting for the ability to generate gossip, I couldn't help but think that this one could be more valuable. I got my camera ready as I tiptoed to the entrance of the pavilion.

"Get going!" Heather whisper-yelled to Jax.

"I thought you were coming," he replied.

"I've got to get back to the dressing room," she said.

"No one's going to miss you. You don't go on for, like, an hour."

"What are you, a baby?" Heather asked. "Just go!"

"This is your dumb plan. You go."

Dumb plan? What could *this* be in reference to, I wonder?

Okay, I didn't wonder at all. I knew.

"I don't even care about this stupid play," he added.

For some reason, I got all defensive about that. How dare he make fun of the school show! Where is his Orion Pride?

But Heather was defending the art form just fine at the moment. Besides, I had other things to worry about. A seemingly disembodied hand reached out of the darkness and grabbed me on the shoulder.

"What are you doing?" Sam—who was attached to that hand—asked. Loudly.

"Waiting for my heart to slow down," I said, urging her to be quiet.

"Why aren't you getting Toto back from Heather? She's right there."

"Apparently, Jax is having problems with her dumb plan . . . and this stupid show."

"He called the show stupid?"

"Sam."

"Can't say I disagree."

"Sam."

"What?"

"They're leaving."

Heather and Jax had stopped their fighting and were heading out to the courtyard, with Toto.

"Go back to the dressing room," I said to Sam as I made my way across the Pavilion with my camera in hand.

"Where are you going?" she asked, grabbing me before I could go out to the courtyard.

"Wherever they're going," I said. "They're up to something, and I'm going to find out what it is."

I pulled myself out of Sam's grasp and went out to the courtyard. Heather and Jax were nowhere to be seen. It didn't matter. Unless they both decided to take a lovers' leap off the bluff—one could hope—there was only one direction they could walk. I went that way too.

The Orion Academy grounds can get pretty dark at night, what with all the trees and stuff. Luckily, there was a full moon, so I could see well enough to get to my destination. Once I made my way across the courtyard and the north wing of school, I was rewarded when I saw a dim light coming out the open door to the observatory. I hurried to the doorway, stopping along the edge to take a peek. Toto was inside, sitting up on the metal catwalk like he was waiting for Dorothy to rescue him from the wicked witch. As I took in the situation, another hand grabbed me.

Correction. The *same* hand grabbed me *again*.

SAM!

"Get back to the dressing room," I whispered through clenched teeth. It was, like, five minutes to curtain. Jimmy would be calling places soon. He was probably freaking out this very minute.

"And let you stumble into Jax alone?" Sam said. "He can beat the crap out of you."

I couldn't argue with that logic, so I didn't try. Our shows tend to start ten minutes late, anyway. (The result of parents who usually take more time to get into makeup than our cast does. And I mean both the moms and the dads.) So, technically, we still had about fifteen minutes for her to get back.

"I found Toto," I said with a nod in the stuffed dog's direction.

"How dumb does she think we are?" Sam asked.

"Well, considering you did follow me out here when you should be getting ready to make an entrance."

"You know, I haven't quite forgiven you yet," she said. "Don't know if now's the time to be making jokes."

Forgiven me for what? I wondered. I got her back in the show. Why was I suddenly the bad guy?

"Wait here," I said.

"Be careful."

Like she could have given me any more obvious advice.

I couldn't see anyone inside the observatory, but that didn't mean that Heather and Jax weren't waiting for me on the other side of the telescope. I carefully slipped into the room with my camera at the ready. I wasn't sure what to expect, but I was prepared to get some photographic evidence.

I made it to the staircase without a problem. It didn't sound like anyone was in the large room. I guess I should have given the place the once over, but Sam didn't have time. I slowly made my way up the steps, careful to test each tread before I put my weight down on it. All of them were firmly in place. Even the top step had been fixed. Once I reached Toto, I turned to see Sam leaning in the doorway.

I was about to wave the all clear, when the lights when out.

"Bryan!" Sam yelled into the dark room.

"I'm okay!" I yelled back.

But it was too late. Sam let out a yelp as someone pushed her inside and slammed the observatory door shut behind her.

No Exit

The observatory lights came back on. Sam had stumbled a few feet into the room. I still had Toto in my hands on the catwalk. But we both knew the door was locked without even touching it.

Off in the distance, I heard Heather's evil laughter echoing across campus.

"Mwa-ha-ha!"

But maybe that was my imagination again.

I ran down the stairs and joined Sam at the exit. It was locked, naturally. We looked out the glass window in the center of the door, but could only see the dark night surrounding us.

"Heather! Let us out of here!" Sam yelled.

"Come on!" I yelled, pounding on the metal door along side of her.

I couldn't believe I was so stupid to let Heather trap us like that. Too bad we couldn't do anything about it at the moment beyond yelling.

We gave up on the noise before our voices gave out. She slid down to the floor and sat in silence while I looked for some other way out. I ran over to the observatory phone, suspecting the worst. It only took a second to confirm. No dial tone. No way to let anyone know we were there. The show would be starting in a few minutes. There was plenty of time before I went on in the second act. But I wasn't about to let Sam miss her entrance. She opened the play.

You might think that Mr. Randall would hold the show for us. He probably would. But Mr. Randall wasn't running things at the moment. On opening night, the show is turned over to the stage manager. And if you think Jimmy can be anal about where we sit in the makeup room, you should see him when it comes to us taking places.

Once he saw Sam wasn't there, he'd pull Heather onstage. Not that it would require much pulling. Then he'd make a quick announcement that the role had been recast and would raise the curtain before Mr. Randall could do anything about it.

I'm sure Mr. Randall would then rush backstage, but the damage would already be done. The show would go on.

Without us.

Hope would insist on sending out a search party. Sam's mom would probably head it up. But who would ever think to look for us all the way out here?

I gave up on finding an exit and sat beside Sam. Hoping to

lighten the mood, I came up with an escape suggestion. "I guess we could find the switch that opens up the roof and extends the telescope. One of us could shimmy up the telescope, drop onto the roof, and then jump to the ground."

"Go ahead."

I did not like her tone at all.

"Still, I have to say, it was an impressive plan," I said, struggling for conversation. "Heather probably knew we'd come here together. She anticipated that one of us would stay outside. So she had to find a way to force us both inside."

"A true criminal mastermind," Sam said.

"On the bright side," I said, "Heather got us talking again."

"Seems like you're the one doing all the talking," Sam said as she turned away from me.

"We're stuck in here," I said. "We might as well get it all out. Why are you so mad at me?"

Sam looked me over, like she was deciding whether or not she wanted to deal with this now. I guess logic eventually won out. We had nothing else to do at the moment. "You shouldn't have gone to Eric," she said.

"Is that what this is about?" I was glad to finally have some context. "I was doing it for you."

"I don't remember asking you to get involved."

"Friends don't have to ask," I said, basking in my own smugness. I had the moral high ground here. I don't know why she refused to see it. Granted, it would have been easier to see if we were standing under the stage lights, but we can't have everything.

"You only went to Eric because you didn't care if he got in trouble," Sam said. I would have been more impressed by her reasoning if my motivation hadn't been so obvious.

"What do you even see in him?" I asked.

She shot back with her own question. "What do you hate about him?

"He's *so* boring."

"To you, maybe," Sam said. "I know plenty of people who find him quite interesting."

"Of course you do. He's *perfect*. So boringly perfect. And normal. You deserve better than normal. You deserve extraordinary."

"Star soccer player. At the top of the class. Looks that could stop a truck. This is normal?"

"You know what I mean."

"Hardly ever, lately."

How could I put it into words when I didn't even understand it myself? Sure, my hatred of Eric went way back and had more to do with Drew than it did Sam. But this wasn't about that. Honestly. This was about something else entirely. "You deserve someone as unique as you are. He doesn't fit in with us. He's so . . . typical."

"You know, I'm getting a little tired of you always talking about how *unique* we are. How we're the Drama Geeks and that makes us different by definition."

"Well, we are," I insisted.

"Are we? Really?" Sam asked. "Your mom designs outfits for dogs that cost more than my entire wardrobe. Hope writes poetry about a pet that died five years ago. Cindy's posing nude and appearing in Victoria's Secret ads. Heather's going around knocking off the competition for the lead in a high school production of *The Wizard of Oz*. You and me? We're the most *normal* people we know."

"But we're the Drama Geeks," I said weakly.

"And at any other school, people would be staring at us when we went down the halls between classes singing show tunes," Sam said.

"Exactly."

"But it's kind of hard to compete when half the people we go to school with think the hallways are their own personal runway where they show the latest fashions Mommy and Daddy bought them when they jetted off to Milan over spring break."

I wanted to argue the point, but I gave up on fighting logical arguments long ago. Sam was right. We *are* normal. Blandly, boringly normal.

Sure, we know how to turn a phrase. And I'd say that we each have a pretty biting wit. At any other school, we *would* be the eccentric artsy crowd. But when it comes down to it, the only thing freakish about us in comparison with the rest of Orion Academy is that we aren't insane.

Although that didn't explain the overriding question.

"But Eric?" I asked.

Sam shook her head and laughed at me. "Aren't you tired of people thinking that you and I are dating?"

"Well . . . yeah," I said. And for the first time, I realized that was a lie. I didn't really mind. Because as long as people thought we were dating, no one was asking me why I *wasn't* trying to date anyone else. "But it's not that big a deal," I quickly added to cover the revelation.

"It is to me," Sam said very gently. I think she was trying to spare my feelings. "I *want* to date someone and turn heads because I'm dating him. Not because you and I know all the words to 'Suddenly Seymour.'"

"We are pretty good on that one," I said.

Well, we are!

"Have you ever noticed that when people around here look at me, it's not because of my acting? Or even our eccentricities?" Sam asked. "I'm reminded that I'm different every day here. Whether it's the girls asking me where I got my outfit, knowing that it's last year's fashion because it came from an outlet. Or if it's the guys who know they can't take me home to Mother because my mom is only a teacher. So, yes, I like the normalcy that comes with Eric. I *crave* it, in fact."

I thought about what she was saying. It took a moment for it to sink in. I had never realized all those times we joked about hitting Rodeo or made fun of girls wearing outfits with designer names emblazoned on them that Sam wasn't enjoying it the way Hope and I were. I never thought that we were all that different. I guess it's easier to be that way when you don't have reminders constantly slamming you in the face.

Suddenly, I heard how Cindy was all "It's not like she has all that much going for her beside her talent."

Or when Heather was talking about how, "She only goes here because her mom's a teacher."

Sam must get that all the time.

"I'm sorry," I said. "I just assumed . . ."

And there it was . . . exactly what I promised wouldn't happen: a heavy-handed moral on making assumptions about people.

Damn.

Wicked

The silence stretched on for a bit. It was probably the longest time we had ever spent together in one room without speaking, except when we were taking a test. To say this wasn't how I expected to spend my evening would be an understatement. The lockdown was one thing, but knowing how much I had unintentionally been hurting Sam was another. There was only one thing I could say in this situation. "You do realize everyone's going to assume you're after his money."

And finally . . . laughter.

"I am sorry," I said. To be honest, I wasn't 100 percent sure what I was apologizing for: giving Eric such a hard time, being clueless to her social status, or using her as my high school beard. I figured I'd leave it at a simple "I'm sorry" and let her attach it to whatever she wanted.

"Thanks," she said. "Now, how do we get out of here?"

"I'm still leaning toward my shimmy up the telescope idea."

Not surprisingly, Sam ignored me. "It's a shame there isn't more light in here," she said. "There's a chance someone could see the light through the window and come out here."

I jumped up from the ground. "That's it!"

"What's it?" Sam asked as she slowly rose.

"Light!" I pulled out my camera and held it up to the window.

"This is *so* not the time for taking pictures," Sam said. At the same time, she struck a pose in her gingham. "Though I do look fabulous in my costume. It would be a travesty if my fans didn't have some record of me in it."

"Tone it down, Madame Egotistia," I said as I took a sample picture of the door. The camera I used had red eye-reduction, so it ran a series of flashes before the actual flash. The bright light lit up the observatory and, more importantly, spilled out the small window.

"Brilliant!" Sam said.

"We have to do this sparingly," I said. If I started going all flash happy, eventually we'd run out of battery and hope. (That's with a lower case-h-hope. Although if the camera flash helped capital-H-Hope find us, that was okay, too.)

I tried to factor out how long the show would run and then calculate how I could burn the flash off at set intervals. But that was just too much math for my brain to wrap around. Considering we had never even run one act all the way through in rehearsal, it wasn't like I had an idea of how long it took. Not to mention how much Heather's fumbling might slow it down. I figured if I put a minute between each shot and made sure to leave enough battery for the end of the show, we might be okay.

"Now, we wait," I said.

"Oh, fun." Sam slid back down to the floor. "As you know, I'm famous for my patience."

I couldn't blame her for being depressed. It was quite an emotional week for her. She went from having a small leading role, to getting the entire play, to losing the entire play in a matter of days. But just because we didn't have an audience didn't mean we couldn't do the play. As Shakespeare said, "all the world *is* a stage."

I slid my script out of my back pocket, careful not to lose my program.

She looked at me and the script. "Don't even."

Undaunted, I flipped to the first act and prompted her on her opening lines.

"You're kidding, right?"

I repeated the line.

"This is crazy," she said. "We don't even have a stage."

Obviously, she wasn't taking Shakespeare's words into consideration. I stretched out my arms to the room around us. "Think of it as theater in the round." I held Toto out to her and hit her with my version of puppy dog eyes.

The wonderful thing about true actors is that they're always ready to perform. Even if there isn't an audience around. I'm sure that to some people, that's the really annoying thing about actors too. But we really don't care about those kinds of people, do we?

Sam took the prompt—and the dog—and started the Orion Academy Spring Theatrical Production of *The Wizard of Oz*, Observatory Version. We ran through the first act with me playing the guy parts and her playing the girls. Not surprisingly, she knew a fair amount of the girls' lines without having to look at the script. That is one way that she *is* freakishly unique.

Every few minutes I would take a picture of the surrounding landscape and allow the flash to go off. It may have been a waste of time, but at least we were entertaining ourselves.

We worked our way through the first act about as quickly as I imagine they were inside. Actually, we were probably faster. We were averaging several camera flashes per scene, with no hope that we'd be getting out of the locked observatory before classes on Monday. We had just gotten to the point where Dorothy, the Scarecrow, and the Tin Man were about to meet the Lion when there was a banging at the door.

"Sam! Bryan! Are you in there?" a muffled voice yelled from outside.

"Mom!" We both yelled as we bounded over to the glass window, where our savior, Anne, was peeking in.

Thankfully, she didn't bother to ask us the silly question of what we were doing locked in the observatory. She just said, "I'll get the key," and was gone.

"Looks like we'll get you back in time for your act," Sam said, doing a rather poor job of covering her disappointment over missing her act. Not that I blamed her.

"And once we explain what happened, Mr. Randall will put you in the second act too," I said.

"So long as Heather doesn't have any more surprises for us," she said. I couldn't blame her for the negativity. With Heather Mayflower, it was always best to be prepared.

Anne was back in a few minutes with the key and Mr. Randall. Sam grabbed her Toto, and we were off. We filled Anne and Mr. Randall in on what happened on our way back to the auditorium. They both believed us, but without any evidence it was going to be hard to punish Heather for any of it. It was just our word against hers. And she spoke the language of her daddy's money.

Intermission had just begun when we reached the auditorium. We wound our way through the crowd of parents, heading backstage. I thought I heard Eric calling Sam's name, but the noise of the crowd drowned him out. It was just as well. We didn't have time to deal with that, too.

Anne peeled off in another direction as we worked our way through the auditorium. It would have been easier to go around through the empty halls, but this was the direction Mr. Randall had taken.

Being actors who know nothing about subtlety, we burst into the dressing room with just the right amount of flourish. And let me tell you, until you've heard a room go from wildly animated conversations to pin-drop silence merely because you walked through a door, you've never experienced a truly dramatic entrance.

The cast was looking at us with various expressions of

relief and annoyance. Clearly some of the cast still believed Sam was a troublemaker who was just looking for more attention by missing the first act.

Naturally, Hope was the one to break the silence. "It's about time you two got here," she said. "Now, would you like to explain what the heck is going on?"

Hope was surely a sight in her pink taffeta and . . . black steel-toe boots?

I guess she saw me looking at her feet, because she smiled brightly and said, "Found my character."

With a laugh, I let my attention drift from Hope to the rest of the room. Heather was sitting at her makeup station, pointedly ignoring us. She didn't even have the class to look the least bit concerned.

I was momentarily distracted when Eric came into the room. I wanted to remind him that non-cast members weren't allowed backstage during intermission, but it seemed pointless at the moment. The way he moved directly to Sam and took her into his arms was certainly melodramatic enough for him to fit in with the Drama Geeks.

Shortly afterward, Headmaster Collins came into the dressing room and took up a position beside Mr. Randall. I guess Anne had told the headmaster what was going on. I took stock of the room one more time and realized everyone was looking at me for some kind explanation.

Talk about performance anxiety.

Anne was still missing, but I knew it was time to get on with the show. I considered opening with the old "I know you're all wondering why I called you here." But considering we were in the dressing room during intermission, where else would everyone be?

My mind was flooded with information. I couldn't figure out the best way to present it all. It wasn't like anyone needed a recap of the week. The events of the past six days were all that we had been talking about lately. It only made sense to skip to the end.

"Heather did it!" I blurted out. I even pointed an accusatory finger in her direction.

I had expected gasps and maybe even a few people fainting from shock. Some *applause* at the very least.

Yeah. They were still silently staring at me.

"Could you be more specific, Bryan?" Mr. Randall gently prodded. "Please explain what it is you are accusing Heather of."

"She did it all," I said. "Everything. Well, maybe not the lamp falling. But everything else."

Oh, yeah. *Much* clearer.

"Mr. Randall," Heather said calmly as she stood. "I don't know what he's talking about."

Take three.

"I'm talking about locking us in the observatory so we would miss the play," I said. "I'm talking about framing Sam for everything. I'm talking about Wren's 'accident,' and posting Cindy's pictures on the school website. I'm talking about nearly killing Suze. All so you could be the lone Dorothy."

I replayed my accusation over in my head. It still sounded stupid. But maybe that was the brilliance of her plan.

"Headmaster Collins," Heather said. "Weren't we through all this yesterday? There's no evidence to prove I did any of those things."

"Mr. Stark," Headmaster Collins said, immediately raising my own tension level. "We are all well aware of those accusations, but we are looking for proof. Can you prove any of it? Can you prove Heather locked you in the observatory?"

"Well . . . no."

"Did you, at least, see her lock the door?"

"Umm . . ."

"Then I'm afraid my hands are tied," the headmaster said. He didn't seem all that upset by it. I assume that's because he knows my parents aren't nearly as much of a threat as Heather's dad.

I looked at Sam. She was looking at me. Neither of us knew what to do.

"However," Mr. Randall added, "since there is still no evidence to indicate Sam's guilt, I don't see why she can't perform the second act. That is, if she is familiar with the second act."

"Oh, she knows it," Hope said.

All eyes turned to Sam. She looked almost shy as she nodded her head.

"Well, that settles that," Mr. Randall said.

"Wait a minute!" Heather stormed over to Mr. Randall. Somehow, I didn't think she considered the matter settled. "I don't see why I should be punished just because Sam couldn't make her call in time."

"Don't even try it," Sam warned, holding out Toto threateningly.

"Like I'm afraid of you," Heather said. She was stroking her own stuffed Toto in her arms, playing up the role of Evil Heather to the hilt.

The two girls stared each other down. As we all braced for Catfight on a Hot Tin Roof, the dressing room door opened and Anne entered with Jax.

Heather's henchman took one look at the room, saw Sam and me beside the headmaster and burst: "She made me do it!"

"Shut up, moron," Heather said.

"Don't you try to pin this on me," he said. "You were the one who wanted to trap them in the observatory."

As everyone in the dressing room let out an audible gasp, Heather dropped her Toto and bolted out the door.

"Where's she running?" Sam asked.

"Fleeing the country?" I suggested with a shrug.

I ran out the door after her, grabbing Toto on the way. (The Fleischmans did me a favor. I wasn't going to repay them by letting one of their creations get all dirty.)

Heather was already halfway down the empty hall when I got out there. I had no clue where she was going, but I wasn't about to give her time to escape so she could plot a way out of this mess. I silently apologized to the Fleischman Brothers and flung Toto at her head with all my might.

He landed somewhere around her feet. But the stuffed dog still managed to trip her up, sending her sprawling to the ground.

Ding-dong, the witch was dead. Well . . . maybe just stunned a little.

Everyone poured out of the dressing room to find Heather on the floor. She glared at me with a level of hatred I suspect she usually reserves for her sister.

Headmaster Collins took Jax and Heather by the arms. "I think we should go to my office." He then looked at Heather. "Then I'll have a private word with your father."

At that, the entire cast broke into applause.

"We got her, my pretty," Sam said to me as the applause died down.

"And her little dog, too," I added, picking up the stuffed Toto.

As we shared a laugh, Hope smacked us both in the backs of our heads.

All's Well That Ends Well

After all that, you'll probably be shocked to learn that the second act started pretty close to on time. It went off nearly without a hitch. The cast kicked it up a notch with Sam in the role. Hope was excellent with her kick-ass Glinda. And Tasha's flyaway exit in the balloon basket got a full minute of applause.

Sam was brilliant, as expected. She had all her lines down and even covered for me when I dropped one. The jitterbug wasn't as much of a dance number as it could have been, but you should have heard the girl sing. All in all, it was a stellar performance.

Nobody seemed to question why Sam was in the second act when she was supposed to be in the first. In fact, my parents later told me that they hadn't even noticed that anything was wrong with the play. Other than Heather's lackluster performance in the first act, that is.

"Lackluster" was their word, not mine. Nor was it anyone else's in the cast. That night at the cast party I heard many other words to describe Heather's acting. Most of them are not printable here. But before we got to the party, there was one more thing that needed to be done.

Sam got a standing ovation during the curtain call. I was glad to see Wren and Suze in the front row yelling at the top of their voices. I guess Cynthia was still in New York in her underwear. Heather's sister, Holly, was right beside them, though. She looked more annoyed than anything. I could understand it. She had had a tough week. Almost as tough as her sister's.

The warm embrace from the audience was almost the perfect way to end the show. But I had a much better idea.

When Mr. Randall got up on stage to give his curtain speech, I pulled him aside to make a suggestion. I wasn't sure if he'd heard me over the noise, but I was hopeful.

Mr. Randall stepped center stage and took up the microphone. "Parents, faculty, students, friends . . . paparazzi," he said addressing the hushed crowd and flashing cameras. "As many of you know, this has been a trying week for our little drama club. But I think we managed to pull off a good one here." The audience went wild again. "There are so many people to thank, and so many things to say right now, but it's late and we all want to get to the cast party." This time, everyone in the audience *and* onstage burst into applause.

During the break in his speech, Mr. Randall looked at me and smiled. He *did* hear me. "But before that," he continued.

"Due to an unusual set of circumstances that would take forever to explain, we did a little switcheroo with casting this evening. And because of that, I feel, we all missed out what could have been one of the highlights of our production. Ladies and gentlemen, if you would permit us to delay the party for a few extra minutes, I'd like to see if we could convince our remaining Dorothy to sing her rendition of 'Over the Rainbow.'"

Sam did an actual double take, from Mr. Randall to me to Mr. Randall again. She didn't even have time to protest before the audience went absolutely insane. I could even see Eric jumping up and down as he cheered. Apparently, Heather had butchered the song during the show, so they were probably looking for a good rendition.

Sam looked embarrassed, but that didn't stop her from stepping out of the crowded cast. And here's why Jimmy is the best stage manager any high school production has ever seen. Nobody even noticed when he left the stage and ran back to the soundboard, but wouldn't you know that as soon as Sam stepped up to the mic, the first few notes of the song were coming over the sound system.

There was only one word to describe the performance: *Flawless.*

In theater, there is one sure way to tell when you've captured your audience. It's not by applause, it's by silence. Once Sam let go of the last note, there was not a sound in all of Hall Hall. Not a clap. Not even a breath. Everyone was overwhelmed by the pure beauty of her voice.

Then the entire place erupted.

I would love to stop things here with the happy ending. That would be such an old-school musical way to end things. I would add on a tag to say that Heather and Jax got the punishment they deserved. But this is Orion Academy, not the real world . . . and certainly not a classic from the golden age of Broadway.

Heather's dad was pulled out of the auditorium before the second act had started. By the time we reached curtain call, plans for the installation of the brand-new Anthony Mayflower School Lockers were in place, and Heather and Jax were given a stern talking-to.

Justice isn't swift around here so much as it is negotiable.

The official line was that since there was no actual evidence to prove Heather and Jax did anything other than lock us up in the observatory, they got off relatively easily. Especially considering their crimes included assault and attempted murder. Not that they were really *trying* to kill Suze. I'm willing to give them the benefit of the doubt—and avoid a libel suit—and say that they probably never expected such a violent reaction.

It was more stupidity than felony.

But Suze had already moved on . . . to New York, in fact. That's where she would be spending her summer, thanks to Hope. See, the sketchbook that Hope had stolen from Suze's bedroom? Hope sent it to her mom, the famous fashion designer, Natalie Ellis. The phone call Hope got on Friday was her mom telling her she loved every design in the book. By that afternoon, Suze had an invitation for a summer internship. All she had to do was convince her own mom to let her go.

More than an equitable fee for the work Suze did on Hope's dress.

The other Dorothys were equally agreeable. Wren wasn't interested in pressing charges on the arranged accident since she was suddenly cast as lead dancer in a video for a major star under the Mayflower Music label after her leg healed. And we already know how Cindy—I mean, Cynthia—was reaping the rewards of her "exposure."

Anne was the only one who tried to hold her ground. Heather *was* caught with a stolen test, after all. But Headmaster Collins forced Anne to trade off a failing grade for a punishment of a different color.

Okay, there was one actual repercussion: Heather and Jax were forbidden to attend the senior prom.

And speaking of repercussions, Eric was allowed to play in the soccer finals. Surprise, surprise. There was a lot of talk about suspension from the team or after-practice detention, but it was all forgotten by the time the game rolled around.

The Comets won. The crowd cheered.

Which brings me to the junior prom.

It was fantabulous!

I shared a limo with Sam and Eric and Hope and Drew. Suze came along as my date . . . 'cause I saved her life and all. Even better, she made me a vest, a tie, and a hatband for my fedora to go along with her self-designed cobalt blue dress.

We really stood out among a sea of designer gowns and tuxes, and have the photo to prove it.

Well, there *was* one dress that put our outfits to shame. But Suze had had her hand in that as well. Hope looked positively stunning in her black lace-Chanel designed-Shelley Winters-worn couture dress. Even her breasts looked understated in the classy outfit, beneath the beautiful wildflower corsage in a burst of colors that Drew had picked out for her.

We had a blast. I spent the entire night on the dance floor with Sam, Hope, Suze, and (surprisingly) Drew. I even got in a couple slow dances with Sam as the night wore on and Eric hung to the edge of the dance floor. After all that drama, it turns out that Eric doesn't even know how to dance.

Figures.

The curtain may have come down on the Orion Academy Spring Theatrical Production of *The Wizard of Oz* with me listed as Scarecrow #2, but I guess I was moving up in the cast list of my life. I may not have been the star of this particular drama, but I certainly played an integral part. There's still plenty of time for me to take the lead. This show may be over, but I've still got the rest of my own first act to play out.

And . . . scene.

Orion Academy Spring Theatrical Production
The Wizard of Oz
Cast List

Director
Mr. Terrance Randall

Asst. Director / Vocal Trainer
Ms. Deborah Monroe

Stage Manager
James Wilkey

Dorothy
Sam Lawson A Star Is Born
~~Cynthia Lakeside~~
Heather Mayflower Boo!!!
~~Suze Finberg~~
~~Wren Deslandes~~

Glinda
~~Wren Deslandes~~
Hope Rivera
. . . and her black steel-toe boots!

Auntie Em
Emily Whitsett

Uncle Henry
Hayden Reynolds

Hunk
Shawn Wallace

Scarecrow
Jason MacMillan
Bryan Stark
Hey, that's me! And it's spelled right, too!!

Hickory
Erica Prince

Tin Woodspeople
Trent J. Markus III
Randi Cates

Zeke
Theodore "Teddy" Dougherty

Lion
Jonathan Battles

Miss Gulch
Carol Young

Wicked Witch
Dakota Jane Markus
Linda Robertson

Nikko
Gary McNulty "Monkey Boy"

Professor Marvel
Kirk Weisman

The Wizard
Natasha Valentine

Guard
Madison Wu

Coachman
Van Henderson

Apple Trees
Hilary Huffman
Bryce Tanner

Munchkins
Members of the Ninth-Grade Class

Totos provided by *Fleischman Brothers Animal Emporium*

Encore, encore!
Grab a seat for the next DRAMA!

"SOMETIMES I JUST WANT TO RIP YOUR HEAD OFF, DISEMBOWEL YOU, AND FEED YOU TO THE SHARKS!"

There's a pretty picture.

That dainty line of dialogue came from one of my best friends . . . but not the one I would have preferred hearing it from. Hope was in the process of breaking up with her boyfriend and my *ex*–best friend, Drew. Not that this was anything new for them. At last count, Hope and Drew had broken up at least a dozen times. It's just that there was a definite note of finality in this particular fight. A note that was both sweet and sour at the same time, much like the chicken I was dining on with Suze Finberg as we sat on a blanket while trying not to listen. Or, more specifically, trying not to look like we were listening, while we were listening. Just like everyone else on this section of beach. Not that any of us could have missed it. Hope's voice does kind of carry.

"DON'T YOU DARE BLAME ME! YOU KNOW I DON'T HAVE A PROBLEM WITH IT. THAT'S ALL YOU."

We hadn't quite figured out what they were fighting over, but apparently it was Drew's issue, not Hope's. At least, if her latest outburst was to be believed.

"ALL YOU, BABY!"

Then again, it's not like she was at her most rational at the moment.

"How's the chicken, Bryan?" Suze asked me from our little patch of sand as we watched the dinner theater.

"Tastes like alligator," I said. "And the quiche?"

"Real men would totally eat it."

"Good to know," I said. The party could use a real man or two, as far as I was concerned.

Speaking of not-so-real men, we were sitting on the sand outside Eric Whitman's Mondo Malibu Dream Home. The catering staff were definitely earning their pay, circulating between Eric's house and the Mayflower home down the beach. That's right, the party was cohosted by my old arch nemesis, Heather Mayflower, and her sister, Holly. And yet, I still went. I know. Crazy. But everyone who was anyone was on the guest list. Actually, everyone who went to Orion was on the guest list. How could I not go?

Besides, what else did I have to do? All my friends were there.

The party was split between the two camps with a smorgasbord of delectable delights keeping warm in chafing dishes at both ends of the beach. What? You didn't really expect anyone to actually *barbecue* at the Start of Summer Beach Party? How quaint.

At this end of the party, our host, Eric, was nowhere to be found while his best friend's relationship was going through the wringer. *Nice.* Meanwhile, I was trying to avoid my wondering wanderings since my best friend, Sam, was also missing. Yep. She was still going out with Eric. And I was still having a problem wrapping my brain around it. Then again, the night was young and breaking up seemed to be the thing to do. Which brings me back to . . .

Hope and Drew had been dating on and off for about . . . well, it seemed like forever, but it had been just about three years. I'd love to be able to share some cute-meet story about the first time they ever saw each other, but that would have happened back when Drew and I met her in kindergarten. The only thing cute about that meet was that I looked positively adorable in my first-day-of-school outfit: GapKids from head to toe.

As for how the dating thing started, I'm still not really sure. The two of them had never seemed particularly close while we were growing up. Then one day after Drew and I stopped being best friends, I heard he was going out with Hope. That was later confirmed when I saw them holding hands between classes. Sorry it's not a more exciting story, but since I wasn't in it all that much, how exciting could it have been?

"[CENSORED]!"

On the flipside, the language Hope was using had just gotten very exciting. Too exciting for me to even write here. Sorry. Use your imagination.

Just so you don't go thinking I'm ignoring Drew's part of the fight by just including Hope's dialogue, I'm not. Drew hadn't said much for the past few minutes. And what he had said had been spoken so softly that it was almost impossible to hear. Trust me, Suze and I tried. It wasn't easy. So far we had only managed to piece together the phrase "I'm putting you under a hex." And that couldn't be right. Aside from the fact that Drew didn't really go in for the occult, Hope was fairly religious and took these things seriously. If he ever tried to put her under a hex, she probably would have hauled off and knocked him out. Nope. They had to be fighting about a more worldly subject.

But I have to admit it would be pretty cool if Drew could put someone under a hex.

"Try the crab puffs," Suze said as she handed me one during a particularly quiet exchange of dialogue.

"You can't eat crab puffs," I said, needlessly reminding her of her food allergy.

"I know," she said. "That's why I want you to try one. So you can tell me what I'm missing."

I smiled as I popped a puff in my mouth and gave her a thumbs up. It was a pretty good puff. It was also a pretty good time. I mean, for the two of us—Hope and Drew didn't seem to be having much fun.

"So . . . ," Suze said.

"So . . . ," I replied, wondering where this was going.

"I've had a lot of fun hanging out since the prom," she said.

"Oh," I replied, knowing *exactly* where this was going.

Now that Sam and Eric are a couple and Hope and Drew are—or *were*—a couple, we'd been spending a lot of time hanging out as a group these past few weeks. Never big on being the fifth wheel, I started inviting Suze along whenever we went out. Now, let me be clear about this: I *never* asked her on a date. I *never* in any way implied that I liked her as more than a friend. I wouldn't do that to her. I wouldn't do that to anyone. It's one thing not to mention to my friends the fact that I'm gay. It's another thing entirely to live a lie and use someone else in the process. I can't help it if she jumped to the wrong conclusion.

Can I?

About the Author

Paul Ruditis had small roles in the Northeast High School Spring Theatrical Productions of *Bye, Bye Birdie*, *Grease*, and *Little Shop of Horrors*. Even though it's been years since he last set foot on his high school stage, he still can't get over the fact that the stupid car got a bigger round of applause than the cast when it rolled out onto the stage for "Greased Lightning." Not that he's still bitter over it or anything.

The adorable, delicious—
and très stylish—adventures of
Imogene are delighting readers
around the globe.
Don't miss this darling
new favorite!

A Girl Like Moi

by Lisa Barham

From Simon Pulse
Published by Simon & Schuster

Get smitten with these sweet & sassy British treats:

Gucci Girls
by Jasmine Oliver

Three friends tackle the high-stakes world of fashion school.

10 Ways to Cope with Boys
by Caroline Plaisted

What every girl *really* needs to know.

Ella Mental
by Amber Deckers

If only every girl had a "Good Sense" guide!

From Simon Pulse · Published by Simon & Schuster